I0566650

A Little Clean Fun

A SWEET SERIAL ROMANCE

OTHER BOOKS BY LORIN GRACE

American Homespun Series
Waking Lucy
Remembering Anna
Reforming Elizabeth
Healing Sarah

Artists & Billionaires
Mending Fences
Mending Christmas
Mending Walls
Mending Images
Mending Words
Mending Hearts

Hastings Security
Not the Bodyguard's Baby
Not the Bodyguard's Widow
Not the Bodyguard's Boss
Not the Bodyguard's Princess
Not the Bodyguard's Bride

The Miscellaneous Royalty
Miss Guided
Miss Oriented

A Little Clean Fun

A SWEET SERIAL ROMANCE

LORIN GRACE

WITH HELP FROM HER READERS

CURRANT
CREEK PRESS

Cover Design © 2020 LJP Creative Graphics Photos © iStock

Formatting by LJP Creative
Edits by Camille Swasey

Published by Currant Creek Press
North Logan, Utah
A Little Clean Fun© 2020 by Lorin Grace

All rights reserved. No part of this book may be reproduced in any form or by any means without permission in writing from the publisher. This is a work of fiction. Characters, names, locations, events and dialogue in this book are products of the author's imagination or are represented fictitiously.

First edition: May 2020
ISBN: 978-1-970148-08-4

To All The Members of Lorin's Sweet Romance Readers

THANK YOU FOR ALL YOUR COMMENTS.

INTRODUCTION

AS THE ENTIRE WORLD QUARANTINED, I wanted to do something to uplift others. I don't sing, and my videos are rather random, but I do write. I thought about sharing something I'd written, then I had a silly idea…write a daily (almost) romantic serial with reader input.

I promised my readers the story would continue as long as it took for our imaginary couple to be able to put aside social distancing and kiss. That is exactly what we did. I asked questions, and they responded. Sometimes in polls, sometimes in messages, but always with great ideas, including the title.

This story is unlike anything I've ever attempted before, as I had no idea how long it would be, or what twists would take place. In short, I couldn't even outline the manuscript.

One of my faithful readers, Cami, agreed to edit the day's writings each night. Without her help, this daily serial would never have been posted.

For the readers' understanding, I have listed the original posting dates and questions/answers with each chapter. To preserve the privacy of my group members I have identified them as first initial only and only put some of the most pertinent answers. Remember, many people have the same initials!

PROLOGUE

Posted 30 March 2020:

Lorin Grace I have a fun idea, but I need your help.

I need a name for a female and male in a modern love story not related to anything I have written. I also need job ideas for people who are working from home in this time of quarantine.

Go.

> **M:** Construction estimator. Cade and Julianne.
>
> **T:** Marketing manager, VP sales, tech writer, programmer, web designer, accountant, engineer, architect, travel agent, airline reservations, event coordinator, financial planner, project manager, professor (with online classes), genealogist, editor, fashion buyer, consultant, so many possibilities...
>
> **E:** Marketing manager, VP sales, tech writer, programmer, web designer, accountant, engi-

neer, architect, travel agent, airline reservations, event coordinator, financial planner, project manager, professor (with online classes), genealogist, editor, fashion buyer, consultant, so many possibilities...

CHAPTER 1

Posted 1 April 2020

I STARED AT THE VACANT space in the cabinet under the bathroom sink. The last Wednesday in February, I purchased a 12 pack of two-ply triple-roll toilet paper literally hours before the run on toilet paper began. My roommate and I calculated the rolls would last us until the end of April.

Running out of TP was not a joke. Even if it was the first day of April. Stashed in my purse, twenty neatly folded squares lay hidden in case of emergency. On Sunday, I counted seven rolls when I pulled out this one. I turned the empty paper tube over in my hands, the half-inch by two-inch strip clinging to the glue refused to multiply.

Frantically, I checked the rest of the cupboards in the bathroom, including the one that always stuck. A plunger, several old towels (once belonging to my grandmother), a stash of toothbrushes, toilet cleaner, eight bottles of hand sanitizer, and a rubber alligator. The alligator had been in the same spot for as long as I can remember, relegated to the far back corner because it frightened my younger sister when she was two. I'd missed his smiling face.

He floated on his back during my childhood bath times. I pulled it out for my next bath in the claw-footed tub. Now was one time I needed one of the crocheted doll toilet paper hiders to appear. Grandma had one for every season. I regretted not keeping one perched on the toilet tank.

I ran down the steep staircase to the basement and the tiny bathroom my grandfather once used as a darkroom. Someday I would refurbish the basement of the house my great-grandfather built eighty years ago, after I finished the main floor. Except on Thursday nights when I did my laundry, I avoided the basement and its discarded contents.

A quarter roll of industrial-grade single-ply hung from the hook next to the rusted sink. Hallelujah! Mom once told me angels were my ancestors that had passed on. Apparently, my grandfather watched over me tonight, as no one else could have used the scratchy paper, even if it had been on sale half price.

Twenty minutes later, I scrolled through my apps and contemplated my dilemma. According to the shopping websites and our local Facebook 'buy, sell, trade', not a store in the valley had toilet paper in stock. Even the hidden stash at the hardware store had sold out. On Pinterest I found a helpful pin on making a bidet from a squeezable mayonnaise bottle. My roommate's nearly empty mayo bottle sat in the fridge.

Food was one thing my roommate, Julieanne, left when she packed up her car and returned home yesterday afternoon. She hadn't left my favorite sweater she borrowed for her Valentine's date or my Wonder Woman t-shirt that she wore in a TikTok video last week. It was hard to be mad at her. Jobless since mid-March, Julieanne painted the dining room, cleaned out the flower beds, and organized the treasures in the attic instead of paying her overdue rent. Last night when her mother called saying they had admitted her father to the hospital, with a heart attack, not the virus, Julieanne ran around the house packing as fast as she could, stuffing all of her belongings into her beat-up Honda. I

6

couldn't even begrudge her a couple rolls of toilet paper. I would have taken them if I had to drive 1400 miles. She still could have left one for me.

Maybe the stores would have some tomorrow. If I went out early, I might find a four-pack of generic. After the industrial-grade, which might have been older than my twenty-seven years, generic would feel like the expensive stuff. Most stores reserved the early shopping hours for seniors, and there might not be any left.

Far from solved, I pondered other solutions. I could cut up one of my grandmother's ancient towels. Before disposable diapers, people had washed them out. I could do the same. With no room-mates, who would know? I wasn't expecting company anytime in the next month and I knew better than to take my phone into the bathroom during a Zoom conference call.

Before wielding the scissors or emptying the squeezable mayo bottle, I checked the local trade section of the Facebook group. A recent post caught my eye.

Single man with toilet paper searching for a single woman with hand sanitizer for some good clean fun.

Lorin Grace Should she answer the ad?

   M: In a quippy, fun way.

   B: That's a definite Yes from me. How could she not answer the ad??!!!

   L: After she Facebook stalks him of course.

   (And several other yes comments.)

CHAPTER 2

Posted 2 April 2020

FROM THE NUMBER OF LAUGHING faces and thumbs up, the post must be a joke. But I owned eight bottles of hand sanitizer. If he had toilet paper...I was willing to trade, single or not.

I clicked the button allowing me to ask privately about his toilet paper.

This is stupid. He must be a creeper or worse. I shut my laptop. Tomorrow I'd brave the stores. I only needed a four-pack.

Thursday morning brought another April shower. I put on makeup for the first time in five days and was delighted that despite some binge eating, my favorite jeans still fit. Normally I didn't dress up to go to the grocery store, but this was the first time in ten days I'd been anywhere other than my backyard or an early morning jog. The chain store's parking lot was half full.

My hopes rose as I stood in line to enter the store as customer after customer came out with a package or two of toilet paper in

9

their cart. I rushed to the paper goods aisle. There it was in all its glory—toilet paper, the gold at the end of my rainbow. The man in front of me took two of the packages, leaving two.

I reached for one of the four-packs as someone else reached for the other. We both stepped back with our respective prizes. Triumphantly, I placed my store brand toilet paper in my cart.

I heard a small gasp from behind me. Don't look, I told myself. As always, I didn't listen.

The gasp emanated from a woman whose pregnant form declared her need for the coveted TP greater than mine. Wordlessly, I handed her my prize. She thanked me and wiped away a tear with her sleeve. I purchased eggs, bread, cheese, and a box of yellow chicks as a consolation prize. I don't like Peeps, but I heard they shut down the plant that made them. I could always use them to trade later or give them to my sister when she realized she'd forgotten to buy Easter Bunny goodies for her kids. The peanut butter eggs magically hopped into my cart. I'd enjoy one on the way to my next hunting expedition.

A sign in front of the next store saved me from standing in line in the pouring rain: "NO TP". A similar sign was taped on the door of the next store.

I passed a vacant church parking lot. Was it blasphemous to pray for toilet paper? It really was such a first world problem. Only last Sunday I participated in a worldwide day of fasting and prayer for bigger problems and healing. My lack of TP was such a small problem.

I returned home.

By dinner time, I doubted the roll of scratchy single-ply would last through Friday. And my chances of finding another four-pack weren't great. I opened my Facebook app and checked the status of the TP for sanitizer post. He'd garnered a few dozen more laughing faces and comments from other men hoping for some sanitized fun.

I clicked on his profile. Cade. Nice name, he didn't look creepy, and we had seven friends in common. One of which was a manager at a company I used to work for. Another was a guy that I never unfriended after our second date when we decided we were better off as friends. I didn't know any of our connections well enough to message and ask if Cade was a creeper.

Oh, bad nick-name.

I scrolled through his posts. He'd been posting happy pick-me-up memes and news for the past couple of weeks. Nothing extreme.

I clicked back over to his trade post and pushed the message button. My name appeared above the empty box. I typed before I could lose my nerve.

> **Sierra: I have hand sanitizer. Are you really wanting to trade?**

Soon three dots appeared.

> **Cade: Are you serious?**
> **Sierra: More like desperate.**
> **Cade: You know this was a joke, right?**

Of course, I knew it was a joke. But I had hoped.

> **Sierra: Thanks anyway.** ☺

I put my phone in my back pocket only to have it ping.

> **Cade: If you need some, I can spare 4 rolls.**
> **Sierra: If you are sure you can spare them. I do have a bottle of hand sanitizer.**
> **Cade: Where should I bring the TP?**

Not here. I needed someplace with people around. The grocery store parking lot was too risky. Some other poor soul in need might be watching.

> **Sierra: Chick-fil-A on Main?**

There should be someone at the drive-up.

> **Cade: I can be there in fifteen.**
> **Sierra: Thanks.**

I was halfway down Main before I realized I didn't know what car he drove. I laughed. Who else would park in the parking lot? Dine-in areas were closed.

I pulled in next to a lamppost. Since there was no other car in the lot, I hopped out and placed my sanitizer bottle on the raised cement base. I'd chosen the blue bottle of sanitizer, as it wasn't lemon-scented like my favorite kind, and what guy would want lemon-scented hands?

I slipped back into Gretchen, my faithful VW, and waited. He had three minutes before he would be late and twenty more before the sunset. Meeting a stranger in a dark parking lot would not be worth even the most huggable of toilet papers.

———•———

Lorin Grace: So... They are going to meet. What does Cade look like? Photo or description.

> **R:** I think he should go from Cade the Creeper to Cade the Keeper. ☺
>
> **S:** everal answers were in the form of photos: Chris Pratt, Zach Efron, Chris Evans... I think my readers have a type.

CHAPTER 3

Posted 3 April 2020

THE CLOCK ON MY DASH changed numbers again. Cade was officially three minutes late. With only one Chick-fil-A in town, I doubted he was lost and traffic was less than half of normal. I knew this because while other people celebrated Taco Tuesday, I honored takeout Tuesday.

A blue truck pulled into the lot and parked on the opposite side of the lamppost, leaving a parking space between us. I opened Cade's Facebook profile on my phone to confirm his identity. A man dressed in a gray plaid shirt over a gray t-shirt exited the truck with a plastic grocery sack containing rolls of toilet paper. Same slightly mussed brown hair and lean build. He looked taller than I assumed he was from his profile photo. The couple days' worth of beard growth accented his jaw nicely.+

Stick to your purpose, Sierra. The sack of TP looked good too. He approached the light pole and picked up the sanitizer and tried to set the sack in the same spot. The lamppost base wasn't wide enough.

Cade turned and approached my car. I double-checked to make sure Gretchen's doors were locked. They weren't. Not caring if I offended him, I hit the lock button. The click of the locking mechanism echoed in the car. Three feet from my door, Cade froze. Rats! He must have heard the lock outside too.

He grinned, his smile enhanced his blue eyes. Then he laughed and raised the bag of TP.

No way was I rolling down the window. This was a bad idea. No one knew where I was.

Thump.

Cade set the bag on the roof of the car and stepped back.

My heart rate slowed as he took another step backward.

He held up the hand sanitizer. "Thanks for the trade!"

I waved and gave him a thumbs up.

He continued to walk backward until he reached his truck. I waited until he walked around it and was in the cab before I opened my door to retrieve the paper. The toilet paper was one of the soft-quilted brands. I hugged the sack to my chest.

His truck roared to life. Behind me, I heard the unmistakable sound of a window lowering.

I turned to face him. "Thank you!"

"Any time. Sorry if I scared you."

I shook my head. "I'm just overcautious."

"Aren't we all?"

"Thanks again."

"See you around Sierra." He waved and backed out of his parking spot.

I tossed the bag of TP on the passenger seat and buckled myself in. I doubted he would even want to see me again after my overreaction to him approaching my car. There was a reason I was twenty-seven and dateless. Exhibit A.

The house was too quiet. If Julieanne had been around, she would have laughed at me. If Julieanne was here, she wouldn't have taken the toilet paper and I wouldn't have just made an idiot out of myself in front of a guy in a plaid shirt. I'd watched enough sweet romance movies on TV to know what the plaid shirt meant. He was supposed to be the leading man.

Cade must have had another TP swap after mine, because I wasn't leading lady material.

———•———

Friday morning brought an odd surprise. Snow.

Seriously, could 2020 get any weirder? It wasn't a question I should ask. No one should ask that question.

To shower or not to shower? The 10 am Zoom meeting meant I had to be presentable from at least the waist up, so a shower it would be. And make-up for the second day in a row.

I debated starting one of my hard-earned rolls of TP when I still had a few yards of the single-ply left. If I saved the last bit of single-ply, it would be a good incentive to never run out of toilet paper again. The rest of the roll found a new home in the sticky cupboard. I reached into the grocery sack and pulled out a roll of TP wrapped in tissue paper and tied with curly ribbon. I set it on the counter and pulled out the other three rolls, all wrapped for a party. A reminder I missed out on a potentially fun conversation last night, because of my own insecurities.

He numbered each wrapped roll with a note. Maybe this is why he was late.

> 1. Some cushy for your tushy.

Great potty humor. Maybe the plaid shirt wasn't a sign. I may have dodged an awkward relationship after all.

> 2. Save the tubes to make cardboard Easter eggs.

There was a diagram showing how to pinch the ends of the tube together to form a cardboard egg. With proper rationing, I'd only have one tube by Easter, but I could decorate it.

3. Time to go TP hunting.

I doubted I needed the reminder. It was open season on TP as far as I was concerned.

4. Don't be worried,
Don't be blue,
Call and I'll find another TP roll for you.
Cade 555-9003.

His phone number? He didn't even know me. He might have looked up my profile like I did his. Since we had friends in common, he could see some posts. What if he was better friends with our mutual acquaintances than I was? Did he really want me to call, or was it just a joke to go with his original post.

———•—•———

Lorin Grace created a poll.

Cade makes the next move (he knows her facebook)
9 votes

Sierra calls Cade. 3 votes

Sierra texts Cade 3 votes

Sierra was the one who "creeped" on Cade on Facebook comparing friends. She needs to make the next move! (Added by reader) 1 votes

> **R:** Maybe she waits a day to do anything, and she sends him a text. Just to test that it's his phone. Purely out of boredom. Not curiosity, because that might make her a creeper. ☺

> **T:** They could mention how they met, or what was traded as a way to ensure the numbers/ people are correct.

CHAPTER 4

Posted 4 April 2020

IN GENERAL, I FIND OFFICE meetings a waste of time. On a productivity level, the Friday morning office meeting was a fail. However, seeing everyone's dogs, cats, hamsters, and children brightened my morning. It also left me feeling lonely. My favorite potted violet wouldn't dance around wearing a towel cape or jump on my keyboard. When the meeting ended, I wasn't entirely sure we covered anything on the agenda. Not that it mattered, my boss would send around an email Monday morning changing every decision made during the meeting. And I would ignore it, as did everyone else.

Without Julieanne, the house was too quiet. I'd seen posts that our local shelter had too many abandoned dogs thanks to a rumor that they could spread the virus. A cat could be helpful. I worried about mice in the basement. I spent the next hour surfing the local shelter websites for cats and dogs. When the phone rang, I jumped at the unexpected sound.

Julieanne's photo popped up on my screen.

"Hey, how was the drive and how is your dad?"

"Good and weird. I mean, my Dad is good, and the drive was weird. I stopped at a hotel. I was the only person within about ten rooms. The manager said that they were keeping rooms empty for 2 days between guests and cleaning the rooms twice. There were a lot of trucks on the road, but not many cars. We brought dad home last night. I never thought I'd be happy to say it's only a heart attack."

"I'm glad he is home." I got up from my computer and paced the circle through the connected rooms: dining room, living room, hall, kitchen, dining room ... It was a way to get some steps in.

"Gas was so cheap. If it wasn't so unnerving using public bathrooms, I'd love to do a tour of the USA. But the take in your own TP, wash hands, sanitize hands, wipe gasoline dispenser thing got old fast."

"I can imagine it did." At least she had enough toilet paper.

"Mom says to thank you for the toilet paper. She was down to her last roll. Did you find the one I left you?"

"You left me a roll?"

"With the bag of chocolate peanut butter eggs."

"No— I didn't find either of them." Believe me, if I had chocolate eggs I would know it.

"I left them on ...oh, no." Julieanne's voice faded. "Um, I left them on the front seat of my car ... I just found the other bag of candy."

I laughed. At this point, what else could I do?

"Sierra, I am so, so, sorry! Please tell me you found some TP in the stores."

"Well, about that ..." I told her about the pregnant lady and Cade's post.

"What is Cade's last name? I'm on Facebook now. I know a few Cades."

I sat at my computer and opened up to the Buy, Sell, Trade posts. His post was still up. "Cade Morgan."

18

"Found him. Wow, he is hot. Did you see that water skiing photo from last year?"

"No, I didn't go through all of his photos. I mostly was worried that he might be some stalker wanna be ..."

"Don't tell me you just waved from your locked car window when you met."

"Pretty much?" I winced. "I think he heard me lock my car door too."

Julieanne's familiar exasperated sigh spoke volumes, "Not every guy is Craig. It has been years since he—" Thankfully, she didn't finish the sentence.

"I was more worried because it was nearly sunset and he came right up to my car. He didn't stay six feet away."

"He may have just brushed it off as social distancing then. I have nine friends in common with him. Do you want me to find out more?"

"I was pretty jumpy last night. I'm sure he doesn't want to get to know me better even if he joked about having good clean fun."

I could hear Julieanne typing and hoped she wasn't doing what I thought she was. "My friend Evelyn, you know the Zumba teacher, went to high school with him. She says he is a nice guy. Really funny."

"I figured he had a sense of humor from his post."

"His senior year he gave every girl in the school a carnation on Valentine's Day and paid for them himself."

"That is just too good to be true." I knew too well that good deeds didn't make a good person.

I heard Julieanne typing again. "I think you should reach out to him."

"He gave me his phone number."

"Call him!"

"I don't think I should."

"No, it is perfect. You have a government-mandated distanced relationship. A whole month to get to know him, without actually

19

doing anything together. Isn't that what introverts want?"

She had a point. No hand-holding, no lingering touches, no kissing. Nothing to play havoc with my senses. It might be just what I needed. "I just feel so forward calling him."

"Then message him or send him a friend request. You live in an 80-year-old house, but you don't need to act like you are 80."

Her lecture wasn't new.

"I'll think about it."

I swear I could hear Julieanne rolling her eyes.

"And don't you dare contact him through your friends."

"You're no fun," she whined.

"So you say. But you are still my best friend."

Julieanne laughed. "I'll call you on Monday, and you better have good news for me."

Our call ended, and I returned to my work. I preferred lining numbers up in spreadsheets over dealing with people. Numbers didn't lie.

The problem was that I kept thinking about contacting Cade. And then I'd switch my browser to Facebook. Julieanne was right about the water skiing photo.

Twenty-four hours later I'd started three messages and one text message, watched six episodes of Poldark, and ate all of my Peeps.

I should text him a polite thank-you. It was Saturday night, he'd probably be— or not. There really wasn't much to go out and do.

I walked around my house a few times, as I only had 7865 steps. I should get a pet.

My phone pinged an alert from the messaging app.

Cade: Thanks again for the hand sanitizer.

I debated only a moment before answering.

Sierra: I liked your notes on the TP.

Cade: I promised some good clean fun.

I had no answer, so I sent an emoji. ☺

Cade: Can you guess this movie? ⭐🎬💜🎬

There was an arrow emoji on an envelope, a boy, a heart, and a girl.

The answer was obvious. The question was, should I answer and send a movie of my own?

Lorin Grace Multiple questions...

Does Sierra answer? (What is the movie)

If so, what movie might she use to start this game? (Answer in emojis)

> **M:** Of course Sierra answers. Not sure what movie, though.

> **K:** She needs to answer. I like this movie, but I need a Seattle or Empire State Bldg emoji: 👦❤️👧

> **J:** Yes she answers!! I believe that is You've Got Mail with Tom Hank's and Meg Ryan. If that is that movie, she should also reply with. Tom Hanks movie...maybe he can be their favorite actor. I don't have emoji's for Apollo 13 maybe even Forrest Gump?

CHAPTER 5

Posted 6 April 2020

I SET MY PHONE ON the table and walked away. If only Julieanne were here. She'd snatch the phone out of my hand and send another movie before I could get the phone back. Perhaps that is what I should do.

I sat down and typed.

Sierra: You've Got Mail. 🐕🐱🐱🐱

Cade: Dances with Wolves. You're good at this. 🐺🖤❤️🧑

After I guessed Sleepless in Seattle, we spent the next hour texting back and forth. After ten rounds, I opened my laptop and asked Google for help. Even with cheating, he stumped me a few times.

Cade: I'm running out of movies. How did you get so many?

Sierra: I have a little help from my friend.

Cade: A roommate?

Sierra: Google.

Cade: LOL, the same friend is helping me too. That makes 8 mutual friends.

I sucked in a breath.

Sierra: You looked me up?

Cade: Better safe when meeting a stranger. But we met once before.

I searched my memories. If I had met him before, I would have remembered.

Sierra: I don't think so.

Cade: My roommate Tanner brought you to a BBQ. There was a mishap. I loaned you a t-shirt.

Oh no, no, no, no. Cade had been roommates with the guy I went on two dates with and witnessed one of my most embarrassing moments ever. Not entirely my fault. One reason Tanner and I knew it wouldn't work out is we are both world-class klutzes. Images I'd blocked from my mind replayed.

I asked Tanner to pass me a napkin from the condiment table. He spun with a squeeze bottle of barbecue sauce in his hand. An explosion of sauce covered my face and chest. I stepped, or rather tripped back into the card table holding the two-gallon lemonade jug. Thankfully, it was plastic, so I only had to remove lemon seeds and ice down my back. The worst part was that I had been wearing a white peasant-style blouse and a gauzy skirt. Some guy pulled off his shirt and threw it over me, preventing me from further embarrassment. Humiliation, and the sauce dripping from my face, kept me from looking to see who helped me. The navy shirt covered me to mid-thigh and allowed me to escape the party without allowing everyone to know what kind of underwear I preferred.

Sierra: Did you ever get your shirt back?

Cade: It was nice of you to iron it.

Now would be the perfect time for my phone to flash a low-battery alert. I checked, 64% battery left. Nowhere near dead enough to end the call without lying.

Sierra: Um, the dry cleaners did that.

I couldn't get the stain out. Tanner said it was his

24

A Little Clean Fun

roommate's favorite shirt.

Cade: I shouldn't tell you I wore it to paint my grand-
ma's house last summer then.

Sierra: It wasn't your favorite?

Cade: I can't say I have a favorite shirt. I wore it a lot. And
was very happy to have it back.

An irrational part of me wished that I hadn't given the navy blue shirt back. Not only had it been incredibly soft, it had been the perfect size to wear with my basketball shorts to bed. Not that I had. But I might have thought about it.

Sierra: I don't think Tanner ever told me your name.
I'm sure he didn't introduce you.

Cade: Winking emoji. He didn't.

I had questions about Cade's admission, but I didn't want to ask. Tanner had been such a brief part of my life. We met through a mutual friend who thought two accountants added up to a love match. One very bland date and one coated in barbecue sauce culminated in the text informing me I need to return his room-mate's shirt. I ding-dong ditched the shirt when I returned it so I didn't have to talk to Tanner or the guy who rescued me. Because when I blush it's all blotchy, not cute like in the movies.

I was sure I was blushing now just thinking about things. I needed to answer Cade's last text, but I had nothing to say to change the subject from my humiliations.

Cade: Still there?

Sierra: I am. I just didn't know how to answer.

Cade: Did you know Tanner took a job in California
last year?

Sierra: No, we really haven't spoken since I ruined
the BBQ.

Cade: But you are still Facebook friends with him.

Sierra: I didn't want to be rude and unfriend him, and he
never unfriended me.

Cade: Interesting. Do you keep all your exes as friends?

25

I was not answering that. There was only one guy I listed as an ex in my life, and I had done everything in my power to shut him out of my life. Including changing all of my social media profiles.

Sierra: 2 dates don't really make an ex.

Cade: If I sent a friend request, would you accept?

**Sierra: My feed is pretty boring. Accounting jokes. And
     I don't do selfies.**

He would not find much of my past if that is what he wanted. The icon for a new friend request popped up.

Cade: You didn't say no.

I accepted the request.

**Sierra: Don't say I didn't warn you. I only keep a Facebook
     account so I can follow a few of my favorite authors.**

**Cade: Well, I am glad that we can officially say we
     are friends.**

Sierra: Yup, if it isn't on Facebook it didn't happen.

I yawned. I needed to end the conversation before I started sleep typing.

**Sierra: It's been fun. Thanks for the game. Maybe some
     other time.**

Cade: I have one more for you.

I stared at it. Not a single movie came to mind. Google failed me.

Sierra: I must be tired. I can't come up with anything.

Cade: Hint. It isn't a movie.

Sierra: Still nothing. I'll try again tomorrow.

Cade: Goodnight. Happy dreams.

I continued to stare at the screen for another ten minutes. His last emoji screen had me stuck.

I woke in the middle of the night with the answer.

Or an answer.

Maybe.

Blurry eyed, I opened my phone.

If I was right, Cade asked me on a social-distanced fast food date in separate cars.

I couldn't fall back to sleep.

———•———

Lorin Grace Is Sierra right? How should she answer?

> **C:** I think she's right. She should answer yes with emoji's. I'm bad at titles. Socially Undistanced maybe?

> **M:** Sierra is right and she should answer with a burger and a thumbs up. Now, the question is when. Lunch perhaps?

Lorin Grace Ideas for the title?

> **M:** You Had Me at Toilet Paper

> **C:** Socially Undistanced

> **K:** Though perhaps, stealing another movie title, The (Toilet) Paper Chase.

> **J:** Infectious Affections

> **M:** Just a little clean fun

> **N:** Love In the Time of Covid19

CHAPTER 6

Posted 7 April 2020

SUNDAY STARTED OFF WITH A video chat with my parents and siblings. My younger sister, Hailey, and her husband still wore their pajamas. Hailey pointed out there was no reason to put on a maternity top when no one but family would see her. My brother Brandon and his family dressed in Sunday best. His wife explained that it was an effort to make today different for their three children.

Dad led us in a Palm Sunday discussion and invited us to take part in a world-wide fast on Good Friday. Brandon's kids ran around the room trying to show us how fast they could go. Mom suggested that since her grandchildren might be a little young to skip meals in their fast, that they give up sugar for the day. My sister-in-law agreed.

I read two books in the afternoon while I avoided my phone. The more I thought about my assumption he was asking me on a date, the more I thought I was right. But if I guessed wrong, I'd feel so stupid. Last night's discussion had been embarrassing enough. As embarrassed as I was, I had always thought Tanner's roommate deserved a medal for loaning me the shirt off of his back.

I waited until after ten before opening our conversation on my phone.

Sierra: I have a guess for your last message, but it is silly.

Within seconds the three vibrating dots came up showing that Cade was typing.

Cade: It may not be silly.

Sierra: If I'm wrong, I'

My finger slipped and sent the unfinished post.

Cade:?

Sierra: I'll be almost as embarrassed as I was at the BBQ.

Cade: No one can see you blush.

Sierra: Are you asking me on a socially-distanced date?

Cade: (thumbs up) I thought we could go through the same drive-through and then go park some place and eat our meals together, distantly.

Sierra: Tuesday Lunch?

Cade: You know Valley Burgers on Center? They are local, and I'd like to support them.

Sierra: I like their fries. Good choice.

Cade: Meet you at 12:30?

Sierra: It's a date. Have a good night.

Cade: Goodnight.

I know Julieanne will yell at me for not having a longer conversation. But I get points for saying yes.

———•———

Monday morning somehow felt like Monday despite not going to the office. After working for a couple hours, I took a break and changed out of my pajamas. My brain wasn't in the right place when I wasn't in work clothes. That, and it was far too easy to surf social media when I felt relaxed.

By four, I finished everything in my inbox. Since my position is salaried, I called it a day and searched for a new book to read on my Kindle. I ended up back on social media searching for Cade. I shut my laptop before I could level up to stalker mode.

For dinner, I tried a copycat Disney Monte Cristo sandwich. I either needed a different bread or a deep-fryer. I sat down to read and wondered what Rapunzel would do. Did she really love the prince that rescued her, or had isolation bored her out of her mind?

I won't lie. Tuesday morning brought butterflies. There was something almost forbidden about going on a date, even if we would be yards apart the entire time. For the first time in days, I pulled out my flat iron and created a hairstyle more sophisticated than a messy bun. I loved my hair with beach curls in it. I'd grown my hair out the last few years, mostly because I could, and partially to prove to myself that Craig had lost his power over me. He found super short hair sexy. To please him, a sheer impossibility, I had shaved my hair shorter than Jamie Lee Curtis's shortest cut. When that failed to please him, I bleached the tips of my medium-brown hair. I hadn't realized at the time that his request had crossed the line between a healthy relationship and emotional abuse.

I arrived at Valley Burgers fifteen minutes early. Cade was five minutes late. Leaving me twenty minutes to overthink things. The last seven minutes of "what if he doesn't come" thoughts didn't help those butterflies.

Cade pulled up next to me and rolled down his window. "Sorry, I had a call go over. I didn't text because I assumed you'd be driving."

One point for not texting, but minus two for being late. A teacher once told me people with integrity aren't late. This made twice. I pasted on a smile, not sure how I felt. "That's okay."

31

"I thought we could go up on the hill to eat. There is a church parking lot with a nice view of the valley."

"Sounds good to me."

Cade smiled. It was a very nice smile. "Then follow me!"

He pulled his truck into the drive-through line. Gretchen and I followed. I laughed at his bumper sticker:

I believe in a better world where chickens can cross the road without having their motives questioned.

I was laughing so hard I could hardly get my order out. I'd let the lack of punctuality pass this time.

Lorin Grace Wanted bumper sticker on Cade's Truck to make Sierra laugh! GO!

> **M:** The Lord moves in mysterious ways, but you don't have to. Please use your blinkers!

> **M:** My heart beeps for you

> **B:** I believe in a better world where chickens can cross the road without having their motives questioned.

> **Z:** When I grow up, I want to be an F-150

CHAPTER 7

Posted 8 April 2020

THE EMPLOYEE OPENED THE DRIVE-THROUGH window, and I held out my credit card. He shook his head and handed me my lemonade. "The man in the truck paid for yours."

I glanced in my rearview mirror and saw a minivan with kids bouncing in the back seat and driven by what I assumed was a harried mother. A happy news article I read from a few years ago flashed through my brain. "May I pay for the van behind me?"

The employee leaned out of the window and looked at the van. "Are you sure, ma'am? She ordered four kids' meals plus two other burgers."

"I am sure."

He took my card and shut the window. I saw him talking to another employee who shook her head. A moment later he opened the window and handed me my card and my bag of food. "Have a good day ma'am."

Cade waited at the exit in his truck. I followed through half-empty streets up to the church on the hill. I'd come to this parking lot several times to look at the view.

I parked Gretchen, leaving an empty parking space between us. Cade slid over to the passenger seat and opened his door.

I opened mine and swung my legs out, sitting sideways. "Thanks for paying for my meal."

"As odd as this is, it is a date, and I asked you out."

"Does this feel as surreal to you as it does to me? No offense, but it is the oddest date I've been on. Come in separate cars, get separate meals. Have to experience the whole awkward "how do I start the conversation" fifteen minutes after the start of the date instead of the first three." I reached for my fries and found a cookie I didn't order. On the little white paper bag was a smiley face, and a heart drawn in pen with the word, "Thanks!" written between them.

"Something wrong with your order?" asked Cade.

"No." Setting the cookie on the dashboard, I pulled out my fries. "They do make the best fries."

"I think it is the fact that they cut the potatoes fresh each day. I am biased, as they get them from my uncle's farm in Idaho."

"Are you a farm boy?"

"Only part. I worked summers on my grandpa's farm. I can milk a cow, move irrigation pipe and drive a tractor, but that is all. And you?"

"City girl. Dad always has a huge garden, and we raised chickens a couple of times. What do you do for work?"

Cade wiped some ketchup from his mouth. "I'm a graphic and web designer. You're accounting, right?"

"Yup. I don't have a creative bone in my body."

"Since creative accounting is generally frowned on, that could be a good thing."

I'd heard the joke before but smiled anyway. Soon our meals were gone, and we covered the topics of home versus office work, our favorite celebrity posts...I am a fan of Patrick Stewart reading the Sonnets, Cade preferred the musical performances by various artists from their homes, like Hamilton...and not being able to go places.

"I've always thought of myself as an introvert," I said between bites of cookie. "But the forced isolation makes me want to go out. I've even contemplated getting a dog."

"Your landlord allows pets?"

"I have a loose rental agreement. As long as I keep the house in good repair, the yard neat, and utilities paid, my landlord doesn't care too much. It is kind of a rent to own situation."

"Wow. How did you get that deal?"

"My great-grandfather Wilson willed the house to my Dad. Great-grandpa was 103 when he died four years ago. I took a job here, so dad let me live at the house. I've been renovating it bit by bit."

"After this is over, maybe I can come see what you've done."

"Sure. But it is nothing fancy." I realized he was making plans for almost a month away. We were under 'stay home, stay safe' until the end of April.

Cade put his wrappers in his takeout bag and balled it up. "I need to get back for a meeting at two-thirty. Can we do this again?"

"Yes, it was fun to get out and nice to go on a distanced date."

"Friday lunch?"

"I'm fasting for healing and the end of Covid-19 that day. So maybe something other than food?"

Cade nodded. "I saw a post on Twitter about a Good Friday fast. I think I'll join in. How about dinner Friday night when the fast is over?"

"I'd like that."

Cade checked his watch. "I'd better go. Call you later?"

He was halfway back in his car by the time I responded. I ate the last of my cookie and dusted the crumbs off of my seat before returning home and to my spreadsheets. Friday seemed like a long way away. Maybe I could find something for us to do in the meantime. I wished I was more creative.

—•—

Lorin Grace What should she do?

M: Paint a mural that looks like a stained glass window using painters tape.

C: Photo scavenger hunt through town in their cars?

E: Play an online game together

CHAPTER 8

Posted 9 April 2020

THE REST OF TUESDAY FLEW by. Amazing what a conversation with a real human outside could do. Part of it may have been the fact that it was a date, and one much less disastrous than my last one to the office Christmas Party. I suspect the only reason he asked me was so I could serve as designated driver to our foursome. My date hadn't even noticed when another driver and I switched passengers. I took home the inebriated females, and he took home the males. A ploy that cuts down on office rumor and speculation.

Wednesday, I took a sunrise walk and snapped a few photos of flowers. I needed the reminder proving it was spring. Several dog walkers waved. The dogs tried to come closer than social-distancing standards and sniff me. The walk was energizing and a definite perk of working from home. I never had time for early morning walks before.

By dinner time, the high of talking with Cade was fading. Perhaps it had been the 4 pm video conference call announcing cutbacks and furloughs. Fortunately, I was still a necessary employee, although my previously announced raise became a pay deduction. Again, not as critical in my position as others. A certain sense of guilt filled me. I didn't have a family depending on me or rent to pay. I felt a need to give back but found I was at a loss. I couldn't sew masks, which seemed to be the most popular way of giving back to the community. I scrolled through posts requesting happy photos. I could do that. But would that really help?

I opened the messaging app and sent one of my flower photos to Cade. Maybe it would brighten his day.

A minute later, my phone pinged.

Cade: Aww, you sent me flowers.

Sierra: Oh, I was just sending a spring photo.

Cade: So you didn't intend to send me flowers?

Sierra: Um, there isn't a good answer to that, is there?

Cade sent a photo of a puppy.

Cade: Now we are even. I don't think you want a real dog.

Sierra: That dog is about the kind I should have. I went on a walk this morning and was the only one without a dog. That is when I took the photo.

Cade: I need to get out more.

Sierra: Don't we all? How was your day?

Cade: Normal. Redesigned a website. Swept the floor. Debated jeans vs. basketball shorts.

Sierra: I work better when I am dressed for work. I think it is the mindset.

Cade sent a photo of a pair of tennis shoes.

Cade: Working with shoes off is much better.

Sierra: Agreed. I kick my shoes off under my desk the moment I get there.

Cade: Did you put them on for work today?

Sierra: No.

Our conversation continued for an hour. Just silly things. Stuff that didn't really matter. I didn't tell him about my pay cut or fears of not helping people. I don't know what he didn't tell me. He got a phone call, so we ended our conversation.

———————

A rain shower interrupted my planned Thursday morning walk before it even happened. I didn't want to start work either. Payroll day. This would be depressing. I hadn't processed payroll for a couple of years, but the woman who normally did was sick in bed. She hadn't been to the doctor yet. However, she opted to take a set of sick days. I didn't want to process checks, which for some might be the last full paycheck they received. I turned up my favorite playlist, a work at home perk, and tackled the job, trying only to think of numbers, not names.

At 2:15 my doorbell rang. I wasn't expecting an Amazon delivery. I checked through the window and saw no one at the door. On the welcome mat sat a pot of pink tulips. Attached to the green polka-dot bow was a note:

> I do mean to send you flowers.
> Happy Spring,
> Cade

———————

Lorin Grace Yesterday a reader suggested a photo scavenger hunt. It is going to happen (after tomorrow) I need a list of things they need to find.

Numerous readers listed over fifty items. The winners will be in following chapters.

CHAPTER 9

Posted 10 April 2020

I SET THE FLOWERS ON my kitchen table, knowing if I texted Cade now I wouldn't finish my work. I wondered how he got my address. Because of Craig, I'd searched my name several times, but that was my first name, not my middle name, which I went by now. Cade could have asked Tanner, too. For my peace of mind, I needed to know.

With payroll done, I checked my inbox for other things that I needed to do. Product development wanted new second-quarter projections. I was tempted to send them a GIF of a Magic 8 Ball—it would be as accurate. I refrained, instead responding I would start on Monday. Like the rest of the company, I had Good Friday off of work.

I shut my laptop and used my phone to message Cade.
Sierra: Thanks for the flowers.
I sent a photo of them sitting on my kitchen table.
Cade: Glad I got the right house.
Sierra: How did you know where I lived?

Cade: Tanner pointed out your street one time ... I drove
    down it the other day and saw a "Wilson" on the mail-
    box. I didn't find you on a basic search, but you did
    say your dad owned it.
Sierra: Good deduction.

I hadn't thought about the name on the mailbox. I put remov-
ing the name on tomorrow's to-do list.

Cade: What are you doing tonight?
Sierra: Same thing I plan on for tomorrow. Sorting
    through the items left in the basement. My grand-
    parents didn't throw anything away.
Cade: I wish I could help.
Sierra: Safe time to offer. ☺
Cade: Tomorrow night I'll meet you at the park on 6th
    Street at 6:30. Does that work? Do you like Italian
    or Chinese?
Sierra: Time is fine. I like both. Not fond of super hot food.
Cade: See you tomorrow.

———

Two boxes in and obsolete kitchen gadgets distracted me. A pyramid-shaped grater type object turned out to be a stovetop toaster when I ran a search on the photo I took. Apparently, collectors still wanted them. It had to work better than my electric one that constantly burned my toast on one end.

Instead of eating lunch, I opened my Bible and read several New Testament passages about Christ's last hours. I prayed for Divine intervention and relief from Covid-19 for the entire world, for the economy, healthcare workers, and those who were suffering. I prayed for miracles. I prayed for my mother's friend's husband who had been in ICU for 24 days fighting the virus. For a friend's dance partner in a New York City hospital, and a co-worker recovering at home. Each morning and night I'd included those things in my prayers, but having missed two meals, the fervency of my prayers increased. As the day continued, I found I was always thinking with a prayer in my heart.

Before dressing for dinner, I knelt and prayed again. If ever the world needed God, it was now.

———•———

As I drove to the park, an idea for a date formed in my mind. If tonight went well, I wanted to see Cade again. I needed to ask him out this time.

Cade waited next to his truck holding two takeout bags from a local Italian place.

After I parked he set one on the hood of my car, then walked down one of the paths. I grabbed my bag and followed him to the large bandstand in the center of the park. Cade stood near a TV tray on one side of the bandstand. On the other side was another tray covered with a large white napkin. A single yellow rose lay on a china place setting.

"Welcome to Chez Cade. The best in long-distance dining with a full 12 feet between diners."

I sat at the little table. "It is a very nice place."

"This is a little awkward. I don't normally pray on dates. But it seems like today needs one, or at least a moment of silence." Cade's request caught me off guard. I hadn't prayed on dates either.

"I believe you're right."

"Do you mind if I pray out loud?"

"Perhaps we could stand closer. I feel like we are shouting."

"I have a mask." Cade pulled a fabric mask from his pocket.

I took a scarf from my purse and wrapped it around my nose and mouth. We still stood five feet apart in the center of the pavilion. Cade offered the prayer. It was much like my prayer earlier, minus the personal names. When he concluded, we both stood there for a moment. In some settings, we might have hugged.

"I got us both the sampler plates. I wasn't sure what you like to eat."

"The sampler will be fine."

We returned to our separate tables and talked. Cade had two older sisters and a flock of giggling nieces. I told him about Brandon and Hailey. We discussed the new directive measures and wondered if our date might be out of bounds for them.

"How is your toilet paper supply?" asked Cade.

I laughed. "I have three rolls left, thank you. And yours?"

A blush stole up Cade's cheeks. "I have twenty-four rolls left. I went to my parents' house for Valentine's Day and stopped at Costco on the way home. I bought one of the 30 roll packs, figuring it would last me for a while."

"I usually get those when I go home too. We ran out, and I figured the 12-pack I got at Walmart would last."

"How is your roommate doing?"

"Julieanne is doing well. Her father needs bypass surgery, and she is nervous about it. The doctor is monitoring things in hopes they can wait a month or two." I spoke to her most days, usually leaving messages on Marco Polo.

As we finished our dinners, rain began to dance on the bandstand roof. Thunder rolled in the distance.

"Do you need help to clean up?" I asked. "I can take my dishes home and wash them."

"I didn't think of that. I'm not worried. I can wash them. Put them in your empty takeout bag and set them in the milk crate."

I wrapped them in the unused takeout napkin and the one he'd used as a mini tablecloth so they wouldn't clink and chip. "I'm surprised a guy has china."

"I borrowed a set from my mother two years ago and never returned them."

I so wanted to ask him why. There were few reasons a man would borrow china from his mother.

Cade folded his table and set it near the milk crate. "You can ask me why."

"Why?"

"I was going to use them to propose. Only the night before, she dumped me. Shortly after, I read a sermon on making every day special. So I use the china from time to time instead of saving it for something big."

Why had she dumped him? I'd only known him a week. He seemed nice. Maybe they just didn't fit. "Thanks for making tonight special and memorable. Can I help you carry these things to your truck?"

"If you will take the TV trays and lean them up against the bumper that will save me a trip."

The rain fell harder. "I hate deciding if I should wait out the rain."

"My sisters forced me to watch many movies where a couple caught in the rain is the most romantic moment. Not the same with social distancing."

The cliche kiss in the rain scene. I'd watched dozens of them myself. Sometimes, repeatedly. I glanced at him, wondering if he would have initiated a moment if he had been able to. "No. But if it wasn't for social distancing, we probably would be on a more normal second date." I didn't wait for his reply and made a run for his truck with a folded tray under each arm.

I waited in Gretchen for five minutes. He didn't come. Rats. Had I ruined things? His comment confused me. Did he want romance?

I hadn't asked him out for tomorrow. I opened my phone—only 5% battery.

Cade still hadn't come.

I started Gretchen and drove away.

I plugged my phone in as soon as I got home and opened my computer. My home screen displayed the time. Had the date lasted for 4 hours?

Sierra: I would like to ask you out for a date tomorrow. If you want to go, I need your email address.

An hour later, I crawled into bed. Cade hadn't answered.

Lorin Grace No question today, however, still looking for scavenger hunt items. For tomorrow. :)

CHAPTER 10

Posted 11 April 2020

SUN STREAMED THROUGH MY EAST-FACING windows. Why hadn't my alarm gone off? Rubbing my eyes, before I remembered not to touch my face, I opened my phone to find it was on silent mode. A notification from the messaging app appeared on my lock screen. Cade had messaged me only moments after I crawled into bed. Likely, while I was lying in the dark trying to make sense of the last few moments of our date.

> **Cade: I waited the rain out. I was still in the park at curfew and had a nice chat with a police officer. He didn't believe my story until I showed him the china. I am intrigued with your date idea.**

At the end of his message, he included his email.

Not bothering to dress, I ran out to my laptop and sent him the email I worked on last night.

To: Cade
From: Sierra
Subject: Photo Scavenger Hunt
7:52 am April 11, 2020

Cade-

My date idea is a photo scavenger hunt. Please find these items by Monday. We can meet at the ice-cream parlor on 14th street at a time that works for both of us—they are serving curbside—and discuss your finds. I chose things that you should be able to find at home or outside without going inside of a business. You must take all photos and not lift them from the internet.

1. Easter egg of any kind
2. a dog
3. a small business that is still open
4. a pond
5. a dirty car
6. fire hydrant
7. mechanical pencil
8. permanent marker
9. empty dishwasher
10. 1empty toilet paper roll
11. 1something that makes you smile
12. last book you read
13. stuffed animal
14. view from your front/back door
15. favorite color
16. empty parking lot
17. signs on businesses saying they are open for takeout
18. blooming flowers
19. house under construction
20. favorite childhood photo (May get help from family)
21. breakfast

22. a can
23. fabric face mask
24. something pink
25. a grocery cart
26. a sign thanking healthcare workers
27. a fun window (such as a painted or stuffed animal in a window)
28. a delivery truck
29. chalk art
30. a stop sign
Bonus: a unicorn
Happy Hunting-
Sierra

I put some frozen waffles in the toaster and planned out my day. Obviously, it wasn't fair that I made the list. I owned a stuffed unicorn and had emptied a toilet paper roll last night. I should be able to find the rest of the items by noon. I arranged the waffles on my plate, added a sliced strawberry and a slice of prebaked bacon and snapped my first photo. One down, 29 to go.

I set my phone down and picked up my fork. My phone pinged an email alert.

To: Sierra
From: Cade
Subject: RE: Photo Scavenger Hunt
8:25 am April 11, 2020

Sierra-
It was unclear if you were finding the same items. That didn't seem fair, so here is my list for you. A couple items are the same as on my list. What would Easter be without an Easter egg to hunt for?
1. Easter egg any kind made by you
2. police car

3. a cat
4. a small business that is still open
5. empty playground
6. bird
7. paper clip
8. birthday card
9. dirty dishes
10. full TP roll
11. something that makes you smile
12. last dvd you watched
13. a hub cap
14. view from your front/back door
15. favorite color
16. parking lot with 20+ cars
17. handicap parking sign
18. buds on a tree
19. road construction
20. HS Senior yearbook photo (May get help from family)
21. your lunch
22. a box
23. a bandanna
24. something blue
25. a pothole
26. sign thanking health workers
27. a painted window
28. someone doing yard work
29. a Christmas decoration
30. empty street
Bonus: a penguin
Best of luck-
Cade

So much for the photo of my breakfast. There was only one item on my list I couldn't send. #20. I opened my messaging app.

Sierra: May I have an alternate for #20?
Cade: Why?

I was not ready to explain my relationship with my ex-fiancé, especially his reaction to my five-year high school reunion which culminated in the destruction of all of my yearbooks. My parents had a few photos from my senior photo shoot.

Sierra: I don't have a yearbook. My mom has some
senior photos.
Cade: Close enough. Where am I supposed to find
a unicorn?
Sierra: On a unicorn farm of course.
Cade: Want to play a game tonight?
Sierra: How?
Cade: Online.
Sierra: I'm not into gaming.
Cade: Not the role-playing games. Traditional games.
Battleship, Chess, even mini-golf.
Sierra: Mini-golf sounds fun.
Cade: 8 pm? Bring your own soda, snacks, etc.
Sierra: May the best putter win!

I finished my breakfast and went in search of an empty playground.

———•———

Lorin Grace Thank you, C.J. for the idea of a photo scavenger hunt and all the readers who suggested hunt items. Now it is your turn. Pick a list, either Cade's or Sierra's, and find as many items as you can then post them on either the Cade Post or the Sierra Post. The winning team as of 6 am MST Monday will determine the winner for Monday's chapter.

Chapter 11

Since I rarely went home for Easter Sunday anymore, I can't say that this Easter differed greatly from the last. I bought my favorite candies, colored no eggs, and wore a new dress. Only my family saw the dress in our weekly Sunday online church meeting led by Dad. The walk I took yielded a few more photos for my scavenger hunt list. I hoped to get more Monday morning, but work...

I took a photo of Hello Kitty for my cat and got the photo of the police car on the way to the meetup with Cade. The only item I didn't find was # 26, a sign thanking healthcare workers.

Cade's blue truck was already in the parking lot.

    Sierra: Hey, ready for some ice cream?
    Cade: Yes.

I studied the takeout arrangement.

    Sierra: It may be easier if I order both of them. I was
          thinking we could meet at Canyon Park. There are
          a few dozen picnic tables under the shelter.
    Cade: Is it still open?

Sierra: I walked up there yesterday and it was.
Cade: Works for me.
Sierra: What flavor?
Cade: Raspberry Cheesecake.
Sierra: See you in a few.

I used the online order app. A few minutes later, a worker emerged with my Rocky Road and Cade's ice cream in 2 dishes. I thanked her and hurried to the mouth of the canyon.

Cade sat at a table just inside the shade of the awning. I set his ice cream on the end of the table and chose a table in the next row across from him. "How did your hunt go?"

"Pretty well. I found the unicorn. I didn't find a sign thanking healthcare workers other than on my social media feeds."

"Then I think we tied. I couldn't find a sign either. The newspaper says we only have eight hospitalized in town with Covid-19, but it seems wrong that no one is thanking the workers."

"Maybe people are, but just not with a sign. Food would be more practical."

I finished my ice cream. "I bet you're right. I wonder if there is something we could do."

We tossed around ideas for a while. Neither of us had the money to pay for something for everyone. We did both know a few doctors and nurses.

"What about gift cards?" said Cade. "We could get an assortment of gift cards from the local restaurants and drop them off ding-dong ditch style."

"That would work. We can also trade addresses so if they see us…"

"I like the way you think. Shall we do it tonight?"

"Sounds like a plan." Anything to keep me away from my computer. I knew I would obsess over my newest task, which was literally impossible. There was no way to guess this quarter's sales off of the last two weeks, and previous years were not helpful.

We made a list of the medical professionals we knew, adding a hospital custodial worker that went to Cade's church. Then we decided what gift cards to buy and spit up the list.

"I can print up some quick thank-you cards, and we can meet back here in two hours."

"It will get dark then. How about the Walmart parking lot?" I suggested.

"No table. We need to sort the cards."

"We can meet at the church on the hill. It has a nice sidewalk."

Cade nodded. "I'm just disappointed I didn't win. I was looking forward to picking my prize."

"What would you have picked?"

"Your phone number. You already have mine."

I did? Oh, on the card with the last roll. "That sounds like a good prize. What do I get?"

"What do you want?"

"For you to call me."

Lorin Grace The results of the scavenger hunt were determined by the readers who spent the the weekend decided into teams posting photos. They did indeed tie. Several days later a reader found the last photo thanking medical workers. However, this chapter was finished by that time.

CHAPTER 12

Posted 14 April 2020

DOWN THE STREET A DOG barked. I made it halfway up the driveway when motion detector lights turned on. I sprinted to the porch and set the last envelope on the welcome mat. As I reached for the doorbell, a werewolf inside the house started barking. Okay, not a werewolf, but it sure sounded that way. By the time I reached the safety of Gretchen's front seat, I'd made a new goal to work out daily. I'd made it at New Year's too, but that was like five years ago. No, really it was. Years from now, scientists will write papers on the time warp of 2020.

When I got home, I checked my social media. Honestly, I wanted to know if Cade was home yet. I didn't want to risk calling him if he was being chased by a dog or something.

A message from one of my college roommates waited in my Instagram inbox.

> *Just thought you would like to know Craig is in ICU with Covid.*

No, I really didn't want to know. I didn't wish him dead, just as far away from my life as possible. What was I supposed to do with this? I know I'm supposed to pray for my enemies, but I would have preferred him to be one of the nameless thousands I prayed for each day.

I know prayer works. People were seeing miracles, like my mom's friend whose husband was home after over three weeks of hospitalization. My co-worker was getting better at home. There had been a decline in the US death toll for the past two days, as well as the total global death toll. I knew these were answers to prayer. I knew that I should include him in my prayers. Praying for someone who hurt me? I didn't know how to, even if it was the right thing. Why did she have to tell me?

My phone rang, interrupting my thoughts. I didn't recognize the number, but right now a telemarketer with a vacation to any place would be nice.

"Hello?"

"Hey, how did your deliveries go?" Cade's voice was the best thing I could have heard at that moment.

"You failed to tell me that your nurse friend had a huge dog."

"Snoopy? He is only about fifteen pounds with the bark of a Doberman." Cade's laughter wrapped around me like a warm embrace.

"No, I am sure I heard a werewolf."

"Sorry I didn't warn you."

"I survived. How did your deliveries go?"

"Good. The doctor's teenage daughter was out in front of the house social distancing with a friend in a car. I dropped the envelope at the end of the driveway and told her to give it to her dad. She looked at me like I was crazy. But I didn't hear any sirens, so I don't think they called out the S.W.A.T. team."

I settled in my bedroom like I did when I was a teenager on the phone. "Glad to know they didn't call the police. That would make it twice in one week."

"Maybe for our next date we can do something less likely to get me arrested."

"Like what?"

"Watch a movie together. Wednesday night. Something we can stream at the same time, and laugh on the phone about."

"Do you have popcorn?"

"Yes, do you?"

"I even have an old-fashioned stovetop popper I found in the basement last week."

"Cool. So we're on?"

"Sure. What movie?" I asked.

"That is the problem—thousands of movies—what to watch?"

———•———

Lorin Grace What movie should they see and what streaming service is it on?

> **M:** The Princess Bride on Hearthfire* (your movie network) on demand.

> **E:** Sonic the hedge hog or Onward or God's not Dead 2 on Vudu or something like that.

> **C:** Galaxy Quest.

Lorin Grace Apparently I don't see many movies... I had to look some of them up.

Hearthfire is a fictitious network in both my Artist & Billionaires and Hastings Security book series.

CHAPTER 13

Posted 15 April 2020

TUESDAY, I ENDED UP WORKING late. Surprisingly, not, my boss didn't like the adjusted second-quarter projections. The problem was that some states were extending the shelter in place until the end of May. Others weren't, but they were closing schools, which for many families became the same thing. I found an online version of a Magic 8 Ball. My boss wasn't entertained when I sent it as a follow-up email.

My phone played the ringtone I assigned to my mother.

"Hey, what's up?" Mom didn't call without a reason.

"Not much. You were just quiet on Sunday's call."

"Everyone was. Brandon's Easter Bunny delivered way too much sugar to his kids. I didn't dare say anything, or they might start in with silly faces— round 84."

"So, nothing?"

To tell Mom, or not to tell Mom. If I told her now, she would keep asking me how Cade was. If I didn't and she found out later, she'd lecture me. "Not really. One of my old roommates messaged me last night. Craig is in the hospital with Covid. I put him on my prayer list this morning, but it didn't feel very sincere."

There was a pause on Mom's end of the line. "That must be hard for you."

"Mom, you know it is. I don't wish him dead. I just don't want him near me."

"Do you still have feelings for him?"

We'd been through these questions before. My counselor showed me how my insecurities played into his need to control everything around him. "Same questions, Mom. Still a firm no. I think I feel guilty because I don't feel bad. Does that make sense?"

"After what he put you through, I don't want to put him on my prayer list either."

Maybe I should have told her about Cade after all. "Perhaps I shouldn't have mentioned it."

"I understand. How is Julieanne's father?"

"She texted this morning. He is doing better. She is helping her sister deal with the crisis homeschooling situation. Her brother-in-law is an anesthesiologist, so he moved into her parents' fifth-wheel in his driveway and only talks to the kids through the window or on the phone."

"That must be hard."

"Julieanne is glad he went home. Her sister needs the help more than her father does. She is glad she lost her job here, so she can help."

"How are you and Dad?"

"Other than not getting together with our friends for cards, not that much has changed. Just two old retired people puttering around the house. They have asked me to sew face masks, so that is something to do. Oh, your dad is waving hello."

"Tell him 'Hi', and I love him."

"We love you too, sweetheart. I'll pray for Craig, and that you can find some peace."

That was a huge admission for my mom. When things fell apart the week of our wedding, she was more upset than I was. "Thanks, Mom. Love you too."

On Instagram, I messaged my friend.

Thanks for letting me know. I hope he recovers.

—You know, he has really changed.

That is good.

I logged out before she sent another message. I didn't want to walk down memory lane.

I spent the next fifteen minutes cleaning. Honestly, not that much of a mess with only me. Then I called Cade. "Can you talk, or did I catch you at a bad time?"

"Perfect timing. I was narrowing down my movie choices. Do you have yours?"

"Sorry, I haven't even thought about them. Well, I have, but I haven't looked." I opened to Amazon Prime Movies in one browser tab, and Netflix in another.

"Are you okay? You sound down."

"Sorry, I have been dealing with an old acquaintance in the hospital."

"You've apologized twice so far in this call. No apologies needed. Do you need to talk?"

Talking about an ex-fiance with a current boyfriend rarely works well, but if Cade would bail, I'd rather it be before the first kiss. Which, thanks to the governor, was weeks away. "He is my ex-fiance."

"Oh, more than acquaintances."

"Our relationship wasn't the best. He didn't take the breakup well." Stalked me and left creepy notes, not well. Told my boss I was insane, and spread lies on social media about my infidelity. For the record, I wasn't the one in the back of the car making whoopee with my bridesmaid while I was having my wedding dress fitted.

"Can I assume you are saying that politely?"

63

"Yes? I don't want to explain things. Let's just say I ended up getting a restraining order and moving. I don't wish him harm, but I am really having a hard time praying for him to get well, even though I know I should."

"I won't lie. I am curious. I haven't been in your shoes, but I have an idea of what it feels like to not want to deal with past hurts."

"Now I am curious."

"It is a story for another time. One thing I learned was to try to find a way that the hurt changed me for the better. See that I am a better person or had an opportunity because of it."

I was wiser and more aware of myself. And because I learned what love isn't, I think I am better prepared to recognize the real thing. Of course, I didn't tell Cade that. Way too early to talk about love. "My counselor told me something similar. My relationship was a catalyst in my life. Thanks. That helps. Can we talk movies now?"

"Sure. What movies do you like?"

We finally decided on Galaxy Quest, (which I'd never seen) but changed the date to Thursday. Cade had a client in Hawaii that he was working with, and he was sure their Wednesday call would go past 8 pm.

We chatted until midnight and ended the call with us yawning our goodbyes. He didn't bring up my ex again, and I learned his favorite food.

As silly as it was, I couldn't wait to watch a movie together with him—separately.

Lorin Grace Next date ideas?

M: Joint cooking lesson to make pasta carbonara, or different parts of a meal to share. Painting with a twist—doing their versions of the same painting. Socially-distanced nature walk at a nature preserve.

E: They could tour a museum virtually together or maybe just chat while eating their favorite treats

R: Play pictionary on a Zoom/Skype/ Google Hangouts video call. They could have a virtual talent show. Show something they made, or can perform (i.e. art, cooking, woodwork, juggling, pushups).

C: A game of Would You Rather...

CHAPTER 14

Posted 16 April 2020

THURSDAY NIGHT FINALLY CAME. (WHEN I woke up to snow I wondered...) By then I had watched the trailer and read all the reviews I could find. My popcorn popped, and I sat down and waited for Cade's call. Right on time again.

"How was your day?" he asked.

"Nothing very exciting, and yours?" I wasn't about to bore him with accounting details.

"Good. I got the website done for the Hawaiian company. Ready to start?"

"Popcorn—check. M&M's—check. Soda—check. And you?"

"I have everything. Shall we start?"

It took several tries to get our movies synced. Cade ended up turning off his sound, so it wasn't repeating through the phones.

"Alan Rickman as an alien is just weird."

"I know. I see Snape too."

My soda was half gone when Tim Allen caught a rock monster. The movie got more intense than I expected after that. I jumped when— Oh, spoilers.

"I'd hold your hand if it would help." Cade's voice through the phone made me jump again.

"I may have just buried my face in your shoulder."

"I don't mind."

By the end of the movie, we were both laughing, and I finished all of my popcorn. "That was a good show. I'm glad we picked something that one of us hadn't watched."

"Definitely not the same as a real date. I was serious about holding your hand."

I wasn't sure how to respond. I found Cade attractive and almost too perfect. "I would have buried my face in your side too."

"This stinks, doesn't it? Do you know how bad I just want to say 'jump in a lake' to social distancing?" Cade's voice wasn't exactly menacing, but it held an edge to it. "This afternoon I was on the phone with my cousin. He is a high school senior. I told him I'd help him make a website for his class, but it isn't the same."

"I agree. I see what this is doing to the economy and things. I did the math today, and if I am correct, I projected myself out of a job." More like half the company.

We discussed the economy, those who were suffering, and the news.

Cade paused for a moment. "Sorry, I didn't mean to take us down this trail. I wanted our date to be happy."

"You can't make everything perfect."

"But I want to. I don't want to blow this?" Uncertainty tinged his voice.

This? As in us? "Cade, you don't need to impress me. Just be you."

"But what if me isn't good enough?"

Oh, wow. Was he just pretending? I mean, we all pretended. Maybe this wasn't bad, maybe it was. "Cade you gave me toilet paper, and we have had a couple of fun dates. It's been great."

"I guess my head just isn't in a good place tonight. Thanks for watching with me. Good night."

My phone flashed red to show he disconnected the call. I cleaned up my popcorn and wondered what I should do. Cade had a right to be down. We all did.

I added Cade to my nightly prayers, which pretty much included the entire world at this point. I also prayed for Craig. I needed to let Cade know that his words the other night were the final piece I needed to find peace with my past.

———•———

Lorin Grace What should Sierra do? Note: It did snow at my house.

> **C:** Make Cade some sort of surprise and leave it for him to find.

> **M:** Maybe something silly like a stuffed Spider Man or a Spidey Action Figure-He's a super hero web designer⊠

> **Lorin Grace** FYI I Love you guys! I finished writing a book today and was so out of ideas for this story! You all saved it.... tune in tomorrow :)

CHAPTER 15

Posted 17 April 2020

I ATE THE LAST OF my boxed cereal. I couldn't blame Julieanne for this. I'd been eating it for lunch and a dinner or two when I didn't feel like making anything. While I was eating, I opened Instagram to my messages. I was ready to know how Craig was doing. My friend messaged me again the night I turned off Instagram.

> *When I say he has changed, I mean it. We got married last year. He wanted to apologize for a long time. I never told him I knew how to find you until I took him to the hospital. I knew that it would help him be at peace if he could get a message to you. I have a letter he wrote before we got married. When you are ready, send me your address.*

Wait, what? I looked through her image gallery—not a single photo of Craig. Writing my reply took some stops and restarts.

> *Congratulations. I'm happy for you. I've been praying for Craig. I got some help too. Craig and I were a toxic*

*combination. As difficult as things were, I am thank-
ful for the experience, as I am a better person for it. I'll
keep both of you in my prayers.*

I included my address.

A few moments later, her reply came.

*Thank you. I will let Craig know. It will mean a lot to
him. It has been a rough week. They took him off the
ventilator yesterday afternoon, and he is breathing on
his own again. I should get to video chat with him later
this morning.*

I typed another reply, deleting almost as many words as I wrote.

*If he asks, tell him I forgive him. And I wish both of you
the best.*

I debated about sending it. My friend knew about what happened at the bridal store as she'd been inside with me. I hit send.
It felt good, almost as if I'd lost half the weight I'd gained the last
four weeks. Now if I could do something about Cade. I didn't like
how our conversation ended last night.

My workload was light for a Friday. Since I worked two late
nights earlier in the week, I didn't feel bad about finishing up by
noon. I wanted to surprise Cade with something.

Armed with my shopping list, I headed to my favorite locally-
owned grocery store. They had toilet paper on the shelf. I only
purchased a four-pack so as not to be greedy. On the end cap
to the cereal aisle, the store displayed various types of charac-
ter-based fruit snacks. Not a food I enjoy, but there were some
Spider-Man ones. Last week at the park dinner, Cade mentioned
how an old roommate called him Spider-Man because of his web
crawling and design skills. I grabbed a box. They didn't have
any Spider-Man cereal. Apparently, that wasn't a thing anymore.
But I found a bag of Pretzel M&M's, which he'd mentioned he
liked on one of our calls. The tiny card and party area provided

me with a blue gift bag and a blank card with an old truck on it. I also purchased two gift cards to Valley Burgers at the checkout. (I didn't even know they sold those.)

After putting my groceries away, I put all my gifts for Cade in a bag and added another bottle of hand sanitizer.

Trying to figure out what to write in the card was harder.

> Cade-
> I just wanted to get you something to brighten your life, like you have brightened mine. I kept an extra gift card to Valley Burger. The next date is on me.
> Always,
> Sierra

I debated that ending, and added a smiley face. I thought about turning the tittle on the 'I' in my name into a heart but felt that was too cutesy.

I took the bag out to Gretchen and realized I had a problem. I didn't know where Cade lived. I was fairly sure he wasn't in the same apartment complex he'd lived in with Tanner, but that left an entire town. His Facebook profile was of no help, other than giving me his website. The website had an address on the contact page. I assumed the business was closed, but it was worth a try.

The address was for a newer set of condos. They had glass storefronts on the ground level and apartments on the second floor. The window to Cade's company had shades drawn. There was a printed sign about still being open online. I drove around the building and found Cade's truck sitting in an open garage that must have been under the housing units.

Putting Gretchen in park, I ran to the front of the truck and set the bag on the hood, hoping he wouldn't discover me or put the garage door down. That would just be awkward.

Gretchen and I sped off. Mission accomplished.

Lorin Grace Cade will answer on Monday. (ideas welcome) Cade and Sierra are taking Saturday and Sunday off. ☺

> **M:** He'd better be IN AWE of that really thoughtful gift!

> **J:** I was wondering about her taking the gift to him because she doesn't know where he lives. He definitely calls her up and really thanks her for brightening his day! And tells her that it touched his heart. And he also gives Sierra his home address.

> **T:** Maybe I'm overly concerned that she left it on the hood of his truck, out in the open, where anyone can take it. Is it going to melt? Should she have put it in the bed of the truck? Maybe she should have checked his doors. Heck at this rate, I haven't even gone to my car in weeks. Maybe she should arrange to meet him somewhere just so he will go to his truck.

> **R:** good points. My car has been just sitting there for weeks. But we know he has been places, since he's met up with Sierra recently.

> **Lorin Grace** good points... I guess I wasn't very clear. His store front is in a new building that has apartments above. Finding his truck in an open garage indicated to her that he must live above his storefront/office. Granted even in Utah it isn't wise to leave your garage open, however all the business in that little complex should be small businesses and likely closed. Since she couldn't see the truck from the road,

and assuming Cade has a reason to have his garage open, I think the bag will be safe for the few minutes until he returns. (How authors cover plot holes when they are publishing without a full plot...)

CHAPTER 16

Posted 20 April 2020

I WAITED ALL THE REST of Friday for a response. I broke out the brownie sundae ice cream and watched Bride and Prejudice while texting Julieanne. Bollywood music is the best to lift your spirits. What if the bag got stolen? I was sure I had the right truck, but leaving it in the open garage was risky, even though there really wasn't anyone else around. Who else would have had his bumper sticker? I didn't confide in Julieanne, as she was dealing with her own problems, trying to find the balance between helping her sister and her parents.

Finally, at 11:23 pm, I received a text.

— **Thanks for the bag. I had to run to Idaho. I'll talk more later :).**

A minute later a second text came in.

— **The Spider-Man fruit snacks made me the most popular person here with the under ten crowd.**

From what I'd heard, Idaho's governor's stay-at-home rules were stricter than ours. All I could come up with is that his uncle's farm and his grandfather's farm were in Idaho, so it must be some important family thing.

I kept busy Saturday emptying more boxes in the basement. I found a Betamax video machine with what looked like home videos. I set them aside to digitize them. There were a lot of old videotapes too, including the entire Back to the Future Trilogy. I think my mom's generation was really let down to get to 2020 and still not have flying cars. I was halfway through the second movie when Cade texted.

— My grandma passed away this evening. She decided that she didn't care about distancing and wanted everyone here. She's known for a while her end was near. We had a big family dinner last night, and all of us spoke to her today. I'll be back on Monday. You don't know how much I needed that bag. Can I use my gift card Monday so we can talk? 6 feet away is better than 120 miles or a phone call.

I read his text twice, trying to find the right thing to write back.

Big virtual hugs. I'm glad you can be with your family. Monday burgers work for me. Lunch or dinner? Your choice. Take care. [heart]

—Thanks, Sierra - early dinner at 4:30?
I'll meet you in the parking lot. You are in my prayers.

I turned off the movie and took a bath with the old floating alligator. The toy was meant to hold a bar of soap. I'd used liquid for years. I finally tossed him out of the tub. My sister was right, the alligator was creepy.

Under normal circumstances, I'd give Cade, or any other friend, a hug after losing a family member. How should that work in times of social distancing? I thought of using two pool noodles as arm extenders, but that idea seemed too creepy.

Monday morning, I still hadn't made up my mind about hugging Cade. I'd even looked up Care Bears. I couldn't buy one locally, but I could buy a teddy bear. At lunch, I ran to a local toy store that was still open. (A scavenger hunt discovery.) They carried a wide variety of stuffed animals, and I found a particularly manly teddy bear wearing a bandana. The bear was better than pool noodles. I could hug it, and then toss it to Cade. Would that defeat the purpose of social distancing?

—————◆—————

Lorin Grace created a poll.

Sierra has a dilemma... What would you do? (Add your comments on how to accomplish...)

- Hug 11 votes
- Not to hug 9 votes

> **L:** Unless Cade has specifically been exposed, one hug is probably not going to be the end of the world.

> **T:** I think she should ask him if he wanted a hug and go the direction he dictates, but the teddy bear is nice too.

> **C:** No hug - reasoning: 1. Authenticity (so many other story details and elements have been). 2. Hope and ideas for readers dealing with similar situations. 3. Good example. 4. He has just interacted with how many possible carriers? Not just family, but gas stations and rest stops (lots of public places). 5. Romantic tension.

> **J:** I might be too late for this post, but Sierra should have bought another bear and put them together in a hugging position, she probably would have to do some sewing and then give it to Cade.

Chapter 17

Posted 21 April 2020

IF I HAD A DAISY, I would have pulled out all the petals. I'll hug him, I'll hug him not, I'll hug him... So at 4:15 when it was time to go to Valley Burger, I put an extra face mask in my car along with cowboy bear.

Cade pulled into the parking lot right behind me. The line snaked around and into the lot of the closed store next door. Using Gretchen's hands-free phone feature, I called Cade. "Do you want me to get your order, and I can just meet you up at the church?"

"Sure. A double with cheese—no pickles, large fries, and a Sprite." He pulled out of line. "Wait! What about the gift card?"

"Use it another day."

"I'll meet you up there."

"It looks like I may be about a half-hour. Under normal circumstances, I wouldn't wait this long for a burger."

Cade's rich laughter filled my car in stereo. "I'll see you up at the church."

The line moved faster than I thought it would. There were a half dozen other cars in the parking lot. Cade's truck was at the far end. He stood on the grass where he had placed two camp chairs about three yards apart. He waved and backed up to a tree. I climbed out of the car and placed his order on his chair. Then I did the same with my own order. I debated about what to do with the bear. I'd thought we would be sitting in our cars, and I could just pull him out at the appropriate time. Botheration. Why hadn't I thought of chairs? I left the bear in my car for now.

"I figured we'd be more comfortable in chairs." Cade took his seat.

"I got you extra fry sauce and ketchup. I wasn't sure which one you liked."

"Fry sauce, of course."

We spent most of the meal chatting about little things, like how the rest of the world was missing out since fry sauce was such a regional thing.

Cade dipped a fry in his sauce. "My mom makes the best sauce. She claims the secret ingredient is dill pickle juice."

"I thought it was only mayo and ketchup."

"A lot of people do. They have a similar sauce in Argentina and in Germany."

I laughed. "Who knew there was so much to know about fry sauce?"

"My uncle makes a version with cottage cheese in it and uses it as potato chip dip."

I made a face.

Cade laughed. "My feelings exactly. Maybe if he whipped it smooth, but it is all lumpy and yuck."

"How was seeing your family?"

"Weird. My oldest sister made everyone coordinating face masks for the family photo."

"You mean like family reunion t-shirts?"

"Yup. After the first few hours, we gave up on social distancing. The great-grandkids are all too young to understand. Since about half the family lives on nearby farms, they've already been seeing each other anyway. My mom wasn't so sure and kept wiping everything and everyone down. She made all of us who don't live on the farms promise to go into a fourteen-day isolation."

"Is that why you set the chairs farther than six feet apart?"

Cade nodded. "I don't think I was exposed, but I am selfish and wanted to see you."

"Not selfish."

He told me more about the farm and his cousins. He'd worked on the 2020 website with the one who was graduating. I didn't even attempt to keep everyone straight.

"Do you want any potatoes? One of my uncles is dumping a third of his crop. He is so frustrated. Half the world is starving, and farmers are destroying their produce, milk, and eggs."

I'm not a huge spud eater. "I can take a few."

"Just pull them out of the back of my truck. I brought them down to give to anyone I can."

I had to stand on my tiptoes to see them. Ten was more than enough.

"Is that all?"

"Ten potatoes will last me until June if they don't start growing roots first. I'm not a huge fan of potatoes unless they have been thinly cut and fried."

"You must not have much potato imagination."

"And you do?"

"Ever had potato ice cream?"

"No." Wrong. Wrong. Wrong!

"It is so creamy, you won't believe it."

"I'll take your word on it."

"When this is over, I'll take you to Idaho and we can get some."

I like the sound of when this was over and doing something with him. Even if it was something as unnatural as potato ice cream. "Will your family have a memorial for your grandma then?"

"Probably. We just don't know."

"What is your favorite memory of her?"

Cade leaned back and stared at the sky. "Sometimes she would wait until I was the only one in the room, then bring out a special treat just for the two of us. Sometimes we would sneak off and hide in the shade of the trees in the front yard and she'd have a popsicle for me. Made me feel like I was her favorite. I found out this weekend she did it with all the grandkids and the older great-grands as well. Part of me is sad to realize I wasn't as special as I thought."

"That is amazing. She pulled it off for so long with no one realizing."

"Some girls did, but then grandma recruited them to help hide treats for the younger ones. And grandma's secret helpers never would tell."

Cade shared a few more stories, and the sun started to set over the western mountains.

I took a deep breath. "I really want to give you a hug, but since you promised your mother you would social distance, that is probably out."

Cade closed his eyes and ran his hand down his face. "I did get a lot of hugs this weekend, and as much as I'd cherish one from you, we shouldn't."

"I thought of trying to use pool noodle arm extenders."

Cade grimaced, then laughed.

"Wait just a minute." I ran to the passenger door and pulled out the bear. Now that I held it, I realized that I was touching it. But I touched his Valley Burger bag too … "I figured I couldn't give you a hug, but I could get you a bear." I tossed Cade the bear, and he caught it.

"Thanks." He hugged the bear. "Not the same as you."

"Um, I'm pretty sure that he is a boy bear." Awkward. It never crossed my mind to get a feminine bear. I just wanted something that wouldn't be embarrassing later.

Cade looked closer at the bear. "Nope. See that mischievous sparkle in her eye? She's just been helping out all day on the ranch. Once she gets inside and all cleaned up, she'll put on her best lace hair bow."

"Oh." Note to self find a lace hair bow.

Cade put the bear on his front seat. "Thank you. And I am taking a rain check for that hug."

I folded up my camp chair and put it in the sleeve. Cade did the same with his. We waved and sent air hugs before driving away.

Later, I got a text with a photo of the bear. Cade made a bow out of TP for her.

—14 days and I'll find a way to hug you for real, even if I need a hazmat suit.

I circled May 4th on my calendar and drew a heart.

———•———

Note: Yes, giving a hug won the poll, and I originally envisioned this chapter going that way. However, C's reasoning for her no vote swayed my thoughts. Apparently, essay answers have the win. May 4th we will have a hug to look forward to.

CHAPTER 18

Posted 22 April 2020

TWO DAYS LATER AND I am still sad about missing my chance to hug Cade. I spent half of my work day surfing for hazmat suits. The only ones I found were not from reputable dealers. I needed to get Cade out of my mind. But he kept texting, or calling, or video chatting, and I texted, called, and chatted back.

Being an accountant and curious, I started tracking the time we spent talking to each other in a spreadsheet. Tuesday, we communicated for over six hours. Late-night phone calls were by far my favorite. I didn't have to worry about how I looked, and I could close my eyes and pretend we were in the same room using the speakerphone.

If someone had told me on Valentine's Day, when I was stuffing my face with ice cream and watching the shorter Pride & Prejudice movie, that my next relationship would go on for weeks before we touched, I'd think that they were insane. Just two months ago, we would have held hands, definitely hugged, and maybe kissed after three weeks of dating. I'd never talked to a man as much as I had Cade. I was beginning to think we might run out of things to talk about soon. We'd decided to treat our work at home life as if we were working, so when I got a text from Cade at 3:38 pm, it surprised me.

—What about a double date on Friday?

A double date?

—4 people in 4 different places playing the same game with video chat on.

Sounds interesting.

—I'll let them know. Oh, it is my cousin Justin and his girlfriend Evelyn. He lives in Idaho, and she is in Colorado.

Call tonight?

—Definitely.

I added four minutes to my spreadsheet. Work was slow. What could I say? Two hours remained until the end of Cade's workday. I hunted for something to work on. There wasn't anything. With sales down and furloughed employees, there just wasn't as much work for me. I tried not to wonder how much longer it would be until my cost analyst job was superfluous too. I closed my computer and went for the mail. Maybe I would have a catalog from my favorite bookstore.

I'd forgotten about the letter.

I hadn't even checked to see how Craig was doing, although he stayed on my prayer list.

The white legal-size envelope looked so normal. I'd forgiven Craig. I didn't want to read it. But I did. What if Craig apologized by blaming me? Or worse.

If Julieanne had been here, I'd ask her to read it first.

I couldn't take it into the house to read it. I didn't want to read it somewhere there would be a memory waiting to catch me off guard.

Are you working in your office?

—Yes.

Do you have a mail slot?

—No.

I need a huge favor. Can I meet you at your office at 6? I'll stay outside of the glass.

—Sure. Will you bring me a gallon of milk and a six-pack of Sprite? Are you sick?

—No, I just wanted some.

Sure, anything else?

—No. That's all. Thanks and see you soon.

I took my time getting ready. I still arrived ten minutes early.

I set the groceries next to the door with the envelope and then sat in front of the far window.

Cade opened the door. "So what's up?"

"I got Craig's letter and I am not sure if I should read it. I know it is huge to ask, but will you read it for me first?"

"Do you know how he is doing?"

"No. I haven't looked."

"You're sure you want me to read this?"

"I think so. I've been in a great place and I feel like I've forgiven him. I'm afraid there might be something hurtful in the letter. And I would need to go through the process again."

Cade's face was unreadable. "I'm going to run the milk upstairs to my apartment. Let me think about this." He set the letter on the floor near the window where I sat.

I stared at the letter. Maybe this was a terrible idea.

Lorin Grace Multiple questions today:

1. Should Cade read the letter?
2. Is Craig's letter hurtful?
3. Games for the double date.

M: 1-yes. 2-yes, but the letter explains why. 3-words with friends or scrabble or trivial pursuit.

C: 1 yes. 2 no. 3 the app Psych!

J: 1. yes he should read it. Especially if Sierra asked him to. 2. I would say no. It seems like he is moved on and truly sorry. 3. Sorry no help with that question.

E: 1 yes 2 yes but the letter explains things 3 trivial pursuit or Pictionary or charades

L: 1. Yes. 2. He's genuinely sorry, but there is something in the letter that stings. Cade has to decide whether or not she should read it.

CHAPTER 19

Posted 23 April 2020

CADE RETURNED A FEW MINUTES later. He sat on the other side of the window. "Can you hear me through this?"

"Not well."

Cade held up his phone. Mine rang.

"Can you hear me now?"

I followed his lead and switched it to speakerphone, setting the phone in front of me. "Loud and clear."

He put his hand on the glass. "This is the closest we've been to each other since the night I put the TP on top of your car."

I matched my hand to his. Mine was smaller. He had nice long fingers. "It is the oddest thing, isn't it?"

"It really is." He picked up the letter. "Are you sure you want me to read it?"

"No. I mean yes. I don't know. I've given you a summary of our relationship. I know that I didn't handle things well either."

"Did he ever hit you?"

"No. I thought he might a couple of times, but he never did. And there weren't any #metoo moments. He always stopped when

I said no. I cut my hair for him. I destroyed my yearbooks for him. I dropped half of my friends on social media. But I have some lines I wouldn't cross and those lines I stood up for. I don't think there is anything in the letter that you don't already know about."

"Do you want me to read it out loud?"

"No!" I covered my mouth. "I didn't mean to yell. I don't want to hear his words in your voice. I just need an opinion … It's okay, just give it back."

Cade put his hand on the window again. I matched my hand to his. "Sierra, I wish I could hold you right now. I'll read it."

I bit my lip and nodded.

"Craig has COVID right?"

I gasped. "I didn't even think about the letter having the virus on it."

"I have a big bottle of sanitizer. Do you have some in your car?"

I nodded.

"Go get yours."

By the time I returned to the window, Cade had the letter open. He folded it and put it back in the envelope. "You can read it." Cade opened the door a crack and slid the envelope through. Then, he used his hand sanitizer to his elbows.

I retrieved the letter and turned my back to the window as I read. It was shorter than I expected and dated over a year ago.

Dear Alayna—
I don't know if I'll ever give this to you. I am sure if I send it to your parents' house it will be burned or shredded. I deserve it. I didn't treat you well. I think I knew it then. Sometimes I said jump just to watch you jump. I've been seeing a therapist for a while now. I hope you have too, not that you have any apologies to make. I just don't want anyone to push you around and play with your emotions like I did.

92

I'm sorry about your bridesmaid. I didn't think she would make out with me and definitely not so aggressively. I didn't have the words to break off our engagement, and that was my childish way of ending things. Then, I didn't want them to end...and I was even more stupid.

Don't know if you heard. I'm marrying one of our friends. She made me agree to couples therapy for a year, and I think I'm ready.

So sorry for all the pain I caused.

I wish you the best in life.

Craig

P.S. According to Western Union, there is no expiration date, but there might be a service fee after three years. I figure I owe you the cost of the dress and everything else. Especially since you gave back the ring.

There were ten money orders made out for $1000, each also dated a year ago. It was way too much money. In the end, my parents and I only paid $2000 for the canceled wedding. The bridal store owner had taken pity on me.

I turned to face Cade. "I'm glad I didn't burn it. I should return the money. He gave me way too much, and I am sure his wife will have medical bills now."

"I think you'll need to cash them and have new ones made."

"I think you are right."

"Alayna. That is a pretty name too."

"No one has called me that in a very long time. Mom liked how they flowed together." I put everything back in the envelope and set it on the floor of the car. Like Cade, I used an excessive amount of hand sanitizer. "I'm used to Sierra now. I don't think I'll go back to Alayna."

"I don't know that I could think of you by another name."

I walked back over to the window. "Thank you for helping me." I put my hand on the window again.

Cade matched his hand to mine. "Are you going to be ok?"

"I'm surprised about the money. But I am good. If I hadn't already forgiven him, I might be a mess." It struck me that the last piece of forgiveness had only happened this month because of Cade's advice. I didn't know how to verbalize it. "Thank you."

The two words were not enough, but they were all I had.

"Any time."

"Can I call you later? I'll go see if I can cash these at the Western Union in Walmart and return the money to Craig and his wife."

"Are you returning it all?"

"I'm debating keeping $1000 to give back to my parents. I think they have some healing to do too."

Cade nodded. "I think keeping that much is a good balance. It shows you accepted his trying to make things right. And you may be right about the medical bills."

"I need to call my parents first. So It might be late before I call."

"Operators will be standing by. Did you check to see how Craig is doing?"

I shook my head and opened Instagram.

—Craig is home and recovering. Thanks for your prayers.

I showed Cade the message.

"Call me soon!" Cade stepped back from the window, breaking the not quite connection we had.

"Goodbye." I ended the call and waved.

Chapter 20

Posted 24 April 2020

I HATE THOSE EMAILS THAT come with just a link in them. You know they are phishing emails, and your friend has been hacked. I got one from Cade this morning. He is a web designer; I expected better security. Knowing better than to respond to the email, I texted.

Someone hacked your email.
—What do you mean?
I just got one of those emails with only a link.
—You should open it.
What? That's crazy. It isn't even a normal URL.
—Trust me?

One of the most disliked movie lines is "Trust me." I end up yelling at the character to either run or get over herself. There is no middle ground. I opened the link and I may have let out a little yelp. This was one of those moments when I missed Julieanne. She needed to see this website. Cade built a site featuring Cowboy Bear's life. The funniest photo was of the bear trying to unwind a roll of toilet paper. An Egyptian mummy had a better chance of unwrapping himself.

When did you do this?

—I started taking photos Wednesday night. I took some last night during our phone conversation.

So this is what you do when I end up on phone calls with other people?

—Yup.

It's fun. I can't wait to see what he does next.

—Me too. :) Ready for tonight's games?

I hope so. I can't believe it is Friday. The days are blurring together.

—You've had a couple of busy days.

That was an understatement. One conversation with my parents had not been enough. Dad felt I should give back all the money. Mom thought I should keep more than I planned on. I sent the $9000 back by a cashier's check with a note that took way too long to write. Mostly because my brother, who never liked Craig, kept messaging me.

Just a little bit.

My work message box pinged.

Work calls. See you tonight! (Figuratively)

———•———

At 6:05 pm, my doorbell rang. A pizza delivery guy set a box on my porch and backed up.

I opened the door six inches. "I didn't order a pizza."

"Sierra Wilson?"

"Yes."

"It was paid for, including tip." He waved and ran to his car.

The delivery note just said "Call me." Of course, I called Cade.

"You got the pizza?"

"Yes, you didn't need to do this."

"Pizza is a requirement to have an online game and pizza party.

I've emailed the link to the room. They aren't here yet but we can video chat and pretend we are eating our pizza together."

"This explains last night's conversation about pineapple belonging on pizza." I started my computer and logged in to the website. As soon as I saw Cade, I hung up my phone.

We chatted for twenty minutes before Justin and Evelyn joined us. They also had pizza. We introduced ourselves. Justin and Evelyn were in the same law program. Their university closed down during spring break, resulting in them being in different places. We played boys against girls for Pictionary. The boys won. Cade had some serious drawing skills. The Scrabble win went to Justin first round and Evelyn second round. They both had degrees in English. I dominated in Trivial Pursuit. We chatted for a while, then signed off. I ran to the bathroom. When I came back my screen was flashing funny, so I hit escape. I could hear audio but not see anything.

Cade's voice came through my speakers. "I told you she was smart."

Justin's voice. "And pretty. I like her so much more than Gwen. You are so lucky she—"

I shut my laptop. Cade hadn't mentioned Gwen. I hadn't meant to eavesdrop.

Cade called a half an hour later. "I just wanted to say goodnight. Have you looked at the bear's blog tonight?"

"No. My computer was doing some weird things after the game, so I just closed it."

"What kind of weird?"

"The screen was flashing, and when I hit escape, I heard you and Justin talking. As soon as I realized, I just closed my laptop."

Silence filled the space between us. "You told me about your past. I guess it is time to tell you about Gwen. Only it is a long story that I don't want to start tonight."

"You don't need to tell me."

"I think I do. Remember when you asked why I try so hard? The answer is, Gwen."

"Oh." I wasn't sure what to say.

"Meet me at Canyon Park tomorrow at 10 am and I'll tell you. I want to do this in person."

"I thought you were in isolation."

"Don't worry. I will be. Goodnight, Sierra. Sweet dreams."

Someone needs to inform Cade I don't sleep well when my mind is making up a dozen answers to the mystery of Gwen.

———

Lorin Grace What did Gwen do? Why does Cade try so hard? Ideas?

> **E:** Gwen wanted everything just so and Cade couldn't live up to her expectations maybe.

> **K:** Maybe Gwen was a social climber that pushed Cade to provide her with that lifestyle. When he couldn't do that to her satisfaction, she dumped him for someone who would.

> **P:** Maybe he gave Gwen an engagement ring and the stone wasn't big enough for her. She gave it back to him with a simple gesture suggesting that the stone wouldn't be good enough and neither would he.

CHAPTER 21

CADE MESSAGED ME A PHOTO of a human inside of a zorb.

> **Cade: This was today's plan ...Unfortunately, the ball has to be reflated every ten minutes.**
>
> **Sierra: I've only seen those on YouTube. Where did you find one?**
>
> **Cade: I have a friend who rents them to use on the lake.**
>
> **Sierra: Plan B?**
>
> **Cade: Not yet.**
>
> **Sierra: Let's just go to the park. We can still just sit and talk from a safe distance.**

There was a pause before he answered.

> **Cade: I guess that works.**

Apparently, giving up going over the top was not as easy as me asking.

> **Sierra: See you in fifteen minutes.**

That shouldn't give Cade time to come up with anything else. Unfortunately, it barely gave me time to brush out my hair and put on a clean shirt. Cade's truck was alone at the south end of the lot. I parked three spaces away. I grabbed a picnic blanket and walked to a line of trees. Cade followed a few yards behind.

I spread my blanket in the shade of a tree.

Cade did the same three yards over. "The zorb ball would have almost let us touch."

"Just a week more. The governor has plans to let things open soon, and your self-quarantine will be over. We can make a decision about our social distancing then."

Cade's eyes and smile widened. "I like that thought. I feel like this month has been so long, and that I have known you for so much longer."

"I think that has been because we have talked so much." If my spreadsheet was correct, we logged over ninety-three hours and counting.

"So about Gwen. The short version is we dated for a year. I bought the ring and planned the perfect proposal. The day before, we were picking something up in the mall and walked by the jewelers. She pointed to a ring that she thought was perfect and told me she wouldn't settle for anything rated less than 1.5 carats, colorless, and nearly flawless. The ring I could afford was barely a half-carat. I asked her if the person mattered as much as the ring did. She laughed. I had a long talk with my dad that night and returned the ring. Instead of a proposal, it was a break-up, only she beat me to the punch. Two weeks later, she was engaged, with a 2-carat ring from a lawyer she'd been seeing at the same time as me."

"You didn't realize she'd been dating someone else?"

"We were both busy. I was getting my business off the ground. She was getting an MBA. Looking back, I realized that she chose the times for most of our dates. Then complained if they were too boring. I tend to be a perfectionist, and so I didn't realize that I was measuring perfect by her standards, not mine."

I pushed most of my questions aside. If Cade was going to propose, he must have had feelings for her. We were both old enough that past relationships were a given. "For the record, my only expectation for the ring is that it doesn't fall off. My college friend's husband gave her an adjustable toy ring from the dollar store, as he knew he couldn't afford much. For their fifth anniversary, he finally gave her a diamond. She has the best marriage of all of my friends."

Cade stretched out on his blanket and looked at the sky. "You're serious about not needing things perfect, aren't you?"

"Perfect gets to be too stressful. That was what I was trying to be with Craig. I was trying to match his perfect weather, spoken or implied. I'm not saying that relationships don't involve give and take but that neither person should try to be the other's perfect."

"You are a wise woman."

"I don't mind that you make things fun, but I don't want you stressing out about me needing something over the top all the time. Life isn't a bigger and better scavenger hunt."

Cade rolled over to face me. "A what?"

"A bigger and better scavenger hunt. Each team starts with a new pencil. They go door to door looking for something bigger and better and keep trading up. Have you ever played?"

"I can't say I have."

"My college friends ended up with a couch that way. My team lost." I used air quotes on lost. "We traded for a pink bike with training wheels. The next house we went to there was this girl just the right size to learn to ride. From the old car in the driveway and the textbooks on the table, it was obvious that her parents were college students too. The mom traded a plate of fresh snickerdoodle cookies for the bike."

"I think you may have won."

We talked long enough that we had to move our blankets to stay in the shade. My water bottle ran out.

"Shall we do another movie night?" I asked.

Cade shook his head. "Let's read a book together."

"That could be interesting. What book?"

101

—————•————

Lorin Grace What book should they read?

M: The Princess Bride was a really good read. Jonathon Livingston Seagull is a spiritual read. For the Strength of Youth could lead to some fun discussions.

C: Something that's not too long, but I'm stumped for genre. And it needs to be uplifting. Nothing depressing.

J: Anne of Green Gables. Haha, just kidding!

W: I like the book " who moved my cheese". It's short and fun and gives them a lot to talk about both personally and professionally and in their lives right then.

CHAPTER 22

Posted 28 April 2020

THE LOCAL BOOKSTORE HAD TWO copies of The Princess Bride. I picked them up curbside on my lunch break. We'd both seen the movie and heard the book was excellent, so we decided to determine which was better—the book or the movie. I dropped Cade's book off at his office, waving through the window.

My phone rang.

"The book, I assume?"

"Yes."

"And you pledge you won't read ahead no matter what?"

I put my hand on my hip. "What kind of person do you think I am?"

"The kind of person who reads the last chapter first."

Cade had me there. I was. Except for mysteries. I waited until I guessed the end before I read the last chapter. This was one reason I preferred paper over ebooks. Ever so much easier to read the last three pages of a paperback. "I promise."

"On pain of being banished to the fire swamp?"

"I'm sure I could survive."

"True, but the book version might be more difficult."

"Fine, I won't read ahead for any reason. Satisfied?"

Cade's laughter filled the air. I was sure I could hear it from inside his office as well as through my phone. "Yes. I'll call you at 6:30, and we can start reading."

The rest of the day flew by. A package arrived from Julieanne. She'd marked "Do not open until April 30th" in several colors of crayon. My birthday was this week? I mean, I knew it was, but the month had been so weird that I had more or less lost track. Birthdays hadn't come up with Cade. I didn't know when his was. I checked his Facebook profile. He was one of those annoying people that hid their birthday from the world.

After what he went through with Gwen, saying, "Hey, my birthday is Thursday," seemed super weird. But if I didn't tell him, he might wonder why. There wasn't a good answer to this one. Maybe he was one of those people who checked Facebook and messaged everyone "Happy Birthday" each morning. Considering that he hadn't posted in over a year, I doubted that.

The longest hour of the day was from 5:30 to 6:30. I walked by the book at least ten times. The problem was, there wasn't anything to do. I'd cleaned out another corner of the basement on Saturday. Was a 1945 sewing machine worth anything? I was pretty sure the piles of gingham fabric weren't. When the thrift stores reopened they were going to be inundated.

I called Cade at 6:25. I just couldn't wait any longer.

He answered, laughing. "Is it me or Prince Humperdinck that has you impatiently waiting?"

"The Dread Pirate Roberts, of course."

We read the first chapter. I didn't realize that a simple stew had such ancient beginnings. Now I was craving stew. The second chapter went faster as we waited for the end of the chapter to compare the book to movie. Cade started yawning around nine, so we put down the books and said goodnight.

It nearly killed me not to read again until Tuesday night. Fortunately, it was the end of the month close, so work kept me busy. There just isn't a way to dress up bad numbers. Cade and I grabbed Chick-fil-A, read up at the church parking lot, and watched the sunset. I still couldn't tell if I liked the book or movie better. The book had some things that just wouldn't translate well to the screen. That must be the advantage of the book author working on the screenplay—he knew exactly what to leave out. Of course, we had two-thirds of the book left to go.

We stood ten feet apart, saying our goodbyes.

"Have you looked at the bear's website today?"

"No."

"You should."

I pulled the site up on my phone. Cowboy bear held the hand of a bear in a pink tutu. "You bought him a girlfriend?"

"I figured if I couldn't hold your hand, at least the bear can hold his girlfriend's hand."

Girlfriend? My heart sped up. I would not ask for clarification. "The governor is relaxing more restrictions."

"My mom isn't. I don't think she'd be happy I'm putting you at risk this way."

"Has anyone had even a cough?"

Cade shook his head.

"I'm glad." I waved and slipped into Gretchen before I said anything stupid. Monday we could touch (MAYBE). And I knew holding hands wouldn't be enough.

———— • ————

Lorin Grace How does Cade find out about her birthday? What does he do?

> **L:** Maybe Sierra could be indirect and say something like, "Waiting to read the Prin-

cess Bride every night is so hard for me! Just like not opening my birthday package from my roommate."

C: This is adorable! I started reading Princess Bride over the weekend. I'm still in the first chapter though. Maybe I shouldn't have read all the beginning stuff. I think he happens to see her birthday in his events on Facebook.

CHAPTER 23

Posted 29 April 2020

THE NUMBERS WEREN'T WORKING. THERE had to be a purchase someone didn't record. An hour and a half later, I located it. Just for the record, decimal points matter. I texted Cade.

Late work night tonight. Can we start at 9?

—Doesn't sound fun.

Tomorrow is the end of the month, and I have to have the reports ready to add the last couple of numbers.

This was the worst thing about having the last day of the month birthday. The only day worse was New Year's. Be an accountant, they said. It will be fun, they said. Play with numbers, they said. The college department recruiter forgot to mention that I wouldn't ever enjoy another Christmas break or Halloween until I retired.

—And that is why my CPA is worth every penny I pay. I'd rather create something.

Rub it in. I'll catch you at 9.

Dinner was a bowl of store-brand cereal. I just didn't have the motivation to eat anything else. For the first time this month, I hadn't even bothered changing from my sweats after my morning walk. If Cade attempted a video chat tonight, I'd be on audio only. I wasn't alone; a reporter on Tuesday's Good Morning America was caught with his pants off. My boss gave up on video conferences after his two- and four-year-old children played Captain Underpants in the background of the third, and last, meeting.

Thanks to Cade, I'd done more this month than I had all year. It wasn't so much that I was bored because I hadn't been able to conduct my normal routine, but that I knew I couldn't. My fingernails had grown long without the pool chlorine at my gym damaging them. My bangs finally succumbed to my nail scissors this week.

Julieanne called as I finished up the last of my work. "Happy early birthday. Did you get my gift?"

"It came yesterday."

"Have you opened it?"

"No. I wanted something to celebrate with. My parents sent me a card which will have a check in it."

"What are you doing with Cade?"

"Nothing. I didn't tell him it was my birthday."

Julieanne huffed into the phone. "Why not?"

"Because it feels awkward to just say, 'by the way, tomorrow is my birthday.'"

"If I was there, we would have a party and invite him over."

"Hello, quarantine?"

"You have a big back yard. You should have him over for birthday pancakes."

"I wasn't going to make them. I have some Eggo's."

"What is his number?"

"You wouldn't dare."

"Girl, someone has to look out for you."

"Pass. I'll be fine with my waffles and whatever you got me." My brother and sister weren't likely to remember until the Sunday family call when Mom made some comment that would result in silence and belated birthday cards.

"Fine, then at least open my present now. No, wait! I want you on video phone. Hang up, and I'll call back."

"We only have ten minutes before my call with Cade. We are reading The Princess Bride."

The call disconnected, and just as quick a video call started.

"I love that book. Have you gotten to the bottom of the ravine? I've always wondered what the publisher would send me if I requested the missing kissing scene."

I found the padded envelope she sent. "Nope, not that far."

"Save it for when you two are no longer distancing. I'm sure you can come up with your own."

Acting out a missing kissing scene may be fun, but I was not suggesting it. I unwrapped the paper with painstaking slowness to annoy Julieanne. I finally pulled the lid off the small box. Teardrop earrings, one with a man and the other with a woman inside.

"They're social-distancing earrings! It's you and Cade, in case you can't tell."

I slipped out my tiny butterflies, the ones I always wore. and replaced them with the new ones. "What do you think?"

"Too bad you aren't a blonde."

"Why?"

"Then they could talk to each other by whispering through your ears." Julieanne tugged her blonde hair. She never missed a good blonde joke. I didn't have the heart to tell her it wasn't a good one.

I rolled my eyes at her. "Thank you, they are fun. I need to go now. Cade will call any moment."

Julieanne waved, and the screen went dark.

I noticed just how messy I looked. I ran into the bathroom to brush my hair. Part of me couldn't have a date if I was so sloppy. Good thing, too—Cade initiated a video call. I wished I'd changed my shirt.

Halfway through the chapter, Cade stopped reading. "Do you have people in your earrings?"

I pulled one out and held it up to the camera. "Not actual people. They are social-distancing earrings."

"Where did you find those?"

"Julieanne sent them to me?"

"Why?"

If we were on a regular call, I might have gotten away with lying. There is a reason I don't play poker. My face telegraphs my thoughts like auto emojis on social media. "Tomorrow is my birthday?" I saw myself wince on the screen.

"Weren't you going to tell me?"

"I didn't want to make a big deal out of it."

"Sierra, it is an enormous deal. How many birthdays will you celebrate in isolation?"

"Hopefully, just this one. I was thinking of pushing it off until my half birthday in the fall and not celebrating at all."

Cade grinned. I realized I knew he was scheming.

"It's not a big deal. Understand?"

He shook his head. "Maybe not to you, but to me ..."

"Anyway, back to the book." I held the book between me and the camera, as I'd glimpsed my blush.

"Fine." Cade returned to his place and read. We didn't mention my birthday again.

That worried me.

Earring courtesy of https://www.etsy.com/shop/JetandJones Used by permission of the designer.

Lorin Grace Cade has a birthday to make a big fat social distancing deal out of...What will he do?

L: a bunch of deliveries? flowers, dinner, chocolates? I don't know if you can even order flowers right now -- I still need to find out for Mother's Day.

M: A flowering plant. A pizza for lunch. And a social distancing walk with a fantastic card and a new t-shirt. Wonder what the t-shirt will say?

C: Little surprises, maybe hourly. Definitely dinner. Maybe the birthday pancakes Julianne mentions.

CHAPTER 24

Posted 30 April 2020

—Good morning. Happy birthday. The **bears are celebrating!**

On the website, the bears were enjoying a picnic, complete with a mini-birthday cake.

That's so cute. Thank you.

—I thought of putting up a "Honk! It's Sierra's Birthday!" sign in your yard. But since you had to work overtime yesterday on the end of the month finances, I didn't think you'd appreciate it.

Smart man. I'd been up since six hoping that an early start would mean an early getaway.

—Will you be done by 8 pm?

I better be.

—Social-distancing date in your backyard. Don't worry if you need to be late.

—Oh, and no looking in your backyard after 5 pm. :)

You know, if you didn't tell me not to look, I wouldn't. I haven't since I mowed on Saturday. Now I want to look.

—But you won't.

No. I won't.

I went back to work. Only slightly—read hugely—distracted. At lunch time, the doorbell rang. In case you are wondering, Chick-fil-A delivers, and the frozen lemonade is back. At least it is here. At five, the local delivery co-op, run by all the local restaurants, delivered Chinese with Crab Rangoon. Cade's truck pulled up in the driveway as the delivery person left.

I waved. "Thanks for lunch and dinner."

"How is work?"

"Almost done. Maybe an hour left." At this point I was just checking numbers, making sure the losses I was posting were correct. No one would be happy with the report, but I expected it.

"Text me if you are done early. I'll let you know if I am ready for you to come out."

"What part of not over the top did you not hear?"

"The part that included social distancing. And it isn't over the top. It is the social-distancing issues that make something rather normal, difficult." His grin made me wonder, but I saw nothing large in the back of his truck. So I considered it safe.

Until I got to the fortune cookie. It was custom.

Birthdays are meant to be shared

I uploaded my final report at 7:05 and got ready for our date. This did require makeup and a shower. I'd closed the bathroom blinds earlier, but it was weird showering knowing that Cade was just outside of the window. I texted him a half-hour later.

May I come out now?

—Go out your front door. There is a mask on the rocking chair.

The fabric mask had been made with teddy bear material. I slipped it over my ears and walked around my house. I'm not sure what I expected. Part of the yard had been divided with a rope between two of the old apple trees. Clear, thick plastic hung from the rope. On either side of the plastic was placed a camp chair and a footrest. On my side, Cade placed the same table from the gazebo date. A vase with a single red rose and two wrapped presents. The chairs were placed close to the plastic, side by side, facing the side of my detached garage where Cade set up a portable movie screen.

Cade stood behind a kids' lemonade stand, wearing a mask and gloves. "Welcome to the theater. Tonight's show is, of course, The Princess Bride. Would you like to pick up your refreshments?"

A child's pink sand bucket full of popcorn, my favorite soda, and movie-theater-size candy boxes sat on his side of the stand. I chose my candy and took my soda. Cade took his and walked around the plastic divide where he removed his mask and gloves. "Before the sun sets, we have cake and gifts. If you will lift straight up on the pink box."

A frosted chocolate cupcake with a single candle sat under the box with a packet of matches. Cade set a similar candleless cupcake on his own table.

"You don't want to hear me sing, so try this." Cade tapped a key on his laptop, and the bears appeared on the portable movie screen. They were replaced by videos of what I assumed were various nieces, nephews, and cousins singing happy birthday to me in various keys. The last kid shouted, "Don't forget to make a wish!"

I did. And no, I am not sharing; otherwise, how could it come true?

We sat and ate our cake as I coaxed the identities of the children from him. Cade put his hand upon the plastic. I matched it. Unlike the glass window, I could feel his warmth, but it wasn't the same as touching. "Do you want to open your gift now or after?"

"I think now. When we can see each other."

In the box was a roll of toilet paper. The good stuff. I pulled it out and found writing on the squares.

This square is good for one ice cream cone.

This square is good for one hike in the canyon.

The next 3 squares are good to blot your lipstick.

This square is good for one candlelight dinner.

The list went on. "Did you do this to the entire roll?"

"You'll just have to see."

"I put my hand on the plastic. I really want to hug you."

"There are some squares for that too. You need to find the square for a dinner in a restaurant. They get to open for limited seating on Monday. We can do our first traditional date."

"Can we hold hands under the table?" I asked.

"Do you have hand sanitizer?"

"At least six more bottles."

Cade grinned. "Shall we start the movie?"

I nodded. Cade even played previews to movies before the show started. When our hands rested on the arms of the camp chairs they came as close to touching as possible. Karma better give paybacks on the good side too.

At the end of the movie, Peter Falk described the kiss between Wesley and Buttercup. Cade said something.

"What?"

"I said I want one of those."

"Me too."

Keeping social distancing for the rest of the night was the hardest thing I think I've ever done. We only touched through the plastic barrier as we said good night. Cade sent me inside while he cleaned up. I watched him from the window.

———— • ————

Lorin Grace Monday they get to go to a restaurant! What kind? Also a high thank you to Cami for editing the birthday chapter on her birthday :)

C: I LOVE this! They go to a nice, quiet small business restaurant.

M: Somewhere with fantastic desserts!

CHAPTER 25

Posted 1 May 2020

SATURDAY AFTERNOON WE FINISHED THE book.

"That is a terrible ending. Everyone falling apart." I closed my book.

"I wonder if the book isn't indicative of life. People suffering from their wounds and trying to go on, while pretending it was a 'happily ever after.'"

"Have you always been this philosophical, or is it quarantine?"

Cade chuckled. "I am lying here on my couch, alone, and calling it a date."

I lay on my bed with my phone next to me, attempting to use a hairband as a leg hula-hoop. "Social-distancing dating must bring out the philosopher in all of us. If Wesley and Buttercup marry, then they face an uncertain future. After all, some lawman someplace would be after the Dread Pirate Roberts, making the 'happily ever after' in the movie just as sad."

"Do you think 'happily ever afters' exist?"

"I think they can, but they take work. It isn't like a book where she marries a prince, or a millionaire, or her childhood crush and has a baby in the epilogue. There was a ton of boring stuff in there. That is why authors write epilogues."

"You've thought about this?"

I had no right to be in such a melancholy mood. Ends of good books do that to me. I want them to go on. "I read a lot. I once read a blog about why women shouldn't read romance novels. They set us up for unrealistic expectations."

"Interesting. And what do you expect?"

"In life? Dating? Marriage?" I mentioned the 'M-word' because I wondered if that is what he was asking.

"Marriage?" From his voice, I wondered if he was blushing.

"Hard work. Laughter. Messes. Life is messy. Marriage gives you someone to help you clean it up. I don't think it is the answer to everything, like one of the classic cartoon princesses hoping that Prince Charming will come and rescue them. Though, I didn't mind being rescued by a handsome guy with TP."

"Ah, but the damsel had hand sanitizer. How could I resist?"

We laughed, and the seriousness of the moment dissipated. I couldn't resist knowing his answer. "So what do you expect?"

"Compromise and laughter. I've watched my family, and it seems like the couples who work together and laugh do the best. Plus, not waking up alone. Touch is a big thing for me. I come from a hugging family." He paused for a moment. "It's been killing me not to touch you. I wanted to rip that plastic down Thursday night so I could hold your hand."

"Next weekend I want to watch a movie with you just so you can do that whole "put your arm behind my back for the first time" move."

Cade laughed. "Weekend. I was thinking of a movie on Tuesday. By the way, I have reservations for a restaurant for Monday. With the tables 10 feet apart they all have limited seating, so I couldn't get a table until 7:30."

"Even if it is McDonald's, I want to dress up."

"It isn't McD's, but I know what you mean. I think a sports coat is in order."

"Then I'll wear a dress and heels." I hadn't been this giddy for a date since prom.

"Don't forget your mask."

"I read about wearing masks in the restaurant guidelines. I assume we can take them off while eating. I am bringing my birthday mask."

"Oh, we can have coordinating masks. We can set a new trend for dating couples."

We both started laughing. The phone call lasted for another four hours. We never did decide on which was better—the book or the movie.

Sunday, I decided I needed to tell my family. I waited until there was a lull in the video chat. "So I've been social-distancing dating for the entire month. His name is Cade, and he is awesome."

The predictable questions followed. How on earth could we date? Mom was impressed with the birthday date. My sister was annoyed I hadn't said anything earlier, as, apparently, my dates were more interesting than the latest Netflix fad.

"When do we get to meet him?" asked Dad.

"Not sure about that. Maybe I can invite him over for a video chat soon."

"But that isn't social distancing."

"We are going to a restaurant together on Monday. We've agreed to hold hands."

"What else did you agree too?" My brother made a kissy face. Don't guys ever grow up? Brandon is a father of two.

I rolled my eyes. "And this is why I didn't tell anyone sooner. It's been an amazing month. We have talked so much."

Hailey fake coughed. "You are telling me you haven't touched at all?"

"Not a single skin cell."

My sister-in-law spoke up while she wrestled with her youngest. "That actually sounds like a good way to start dating. No third date kissing pressure."

"Hey, you kissed me on the second date."

I closed my eyes and put my hands over my ears. "TMI, people."

When I put my hands down everyone was laughing. The call finally ended. I spent way too much time choosing my dress and shoes. Tomorrow couldn't come soon enough.

———•———

Lorin Grace Questions, questions. We are winding up. At this point, there will be a kiss, it is inevitable. Are there any questions for me? Do Sierra and Cade need to do/say something that we've missed?

CHAPTER 26

Posted 4 May 2020

THE DRESS STILL HAD THE tags on. I had purchased it a year ago in case I ever had a special occasion. I figured this qualified. Fortunately, the few pounds I'd put on over the month didn't interfere with the fit. Julieanne and I debated about the hair up or down thing forever. I finally decided on an updo with a few wispy locks hanging down. Maybe something to tempt him to take it down? That is always my favorite part of a historical romance. It's probably a reaction to keeping my hair so short for Craig. I loved my long hair and hoped Cade did too.

Fifteen minutes before Cade would pick me up, he texted.

—**Don't forget your mask.**

Got it. It's still unclear to me whether we have to wear it in the restaurant or if that rule just applies to employees.

—**You don't need it in the car.** ☺

I hadn't intended to wear my mask unless they required it. I was more than ready for our first kiss and had spent far more time imagining it than a woman should. Having him pull off my mask to initiate the kiss just didn't work for me. I don't care how many PSAs famous actors film. Not one of them can make a mask alluring. Despite the Dread Pirate Roberts claim that everyone would be wearing masks because they were comfortable, I couldn't agree.

I paced, waiting for him to come. More butterflies fluttered inside of me than I'd had since my first date in high school. My heels pinched. I guessed it was because I hadn't worn shoes much for a month.

It's Cade. You like him, and he likes you. You've been on dozens of dates this month. Calm down. My rational side wasn't winning.

Finally, he pulled his truck into my driveway. I stood in the hall where I could see out of the window, but couldn't be seen in the shadows.

He looked good in the jacket with the blue button-down shirt open at the top. He carried a single red rose. I waited for a beat after the doorbell rang to answer the door.

I couldn't find my voice, so I just smiled. He handed me the rose. Our fingers touched. I wondered if I gathered static electricity pacing, but it wasn't that kind of shock.

I took my time pulling my hand away. "Come in for a moment while I put this in a vase."

Cade closed the door behind him and waited while I ran into the kitchen. I wished Julieanne was there, so I didn't need to leave him. I brought the vase back out with me and set it on the end table. "You cut off the thorns?"

He swallowed. Maybe he was as nervous as I was. "I didn't want you to prick yourself." His gaze swept over me. "I like your dress."

I stepped closer, breaking the invisible six-foot barrier. "You look nice all dressed up too." I took another step. He reached out and took my right hand with his left, our fingers intertwined. We both looked at our hands. There was something magical, almost reverent, about that moment. When I looked up, Cade was already looking at me, his eyes soft and inviting. He raised his other hand to my cheek and tucked the curl behind my ear.

"You wore the earrings."

I leaned my cheek into his palm and smiled.

Cade didn't give me any warning. His lips touched mine in a feather-soft kiss. He lingered for a moment, allowing me to respond before pulling back and dropping his hand to my waist. He rested his forehead on mine. "Now we can both enjoy the evening without wondering."

I brought my free hand between us and rested it on his chest. His heart raced with mine. Wanting to see his eyes, I pulled back. "I knew it would be perfect." I initiated the second kiss, and it was impossibly better than the first.

EPILOGUE

THE INDEPENDENCE DAY FIREWORKS WERE impressive for a small Idaho town. Cade's extended family wandered back down the hill to the farm. Cade took my hand and led me around the back of the hill, where a tree older than the farm stood. We had escaped to this tree several times in the last few days. Four generations of his family had made their marks on the tree.

"Did you see the bear website today?" Cade spread the old quilt we watched fireworks on under the tree.

"Didn't you hear your cousins giggling over the bears watching fireworks?"

Cade sat down with his back against the wide trunk of the tree. "I shouldn't have shared the site with the family. I may have to make a clone site just for us."

"Do you have private things to share?" I sat between Cade's legs with my back against his chest. One more night and there would be a full moon. Tonight there was enough light to illuminate the fields below us.

"Maybe you should decide." Cade handed me his phone and started one of the stop-motion bear videos he'd been making for me.

Cowboy bear walked into a room and stood in front of my Dad. "When?"

"Shh, just watch."

Bear seemed to be talking. Then my dad nodded and shook the bear's hand. The scene shifted to the farm bear carrying a ladder up a hill. He placed it against the trunk of the tree where we sat and carved a heart. Then he watched fireworks with the girl bear. The same scene Cade posted that morning. Only this one ended differently. Cowboy bear pulled a ring box out of his fur and held it out to the girl bear. Girl bear put her paws up to her face, and the clip ended.

I scooted out of Cade's lap and turned to face him.

A slow grin filled his face, and he pulled the same ring box out of his pocket. "Alayna Sierra Wilson, will you marry me?"

My hands flew to my cheeks. I didn't mean to mimic the girl bear, but I did. "Yes! Yes." I may have tackled Cade with my kiss, and he may have bumped his head on the tree. Later he claimed he didn't.

After he got the ring on my finger, he showed me the heart that bear had carved. "It's tradition to carve your initials in the tree when you get engaged. Bear picked out the spot for us." Cade found the heart, and I traced my finger around it.

Cade took out his pocketknife and handed it to me. "You can put your 'S' here."

I didn't have much experience with carving, and by the time I finished the top curve of the letter, I wished that I still went by Alayna. Cade's hand covered mine, and he helped me finish the letter and the downstroke of the '+'. Cade carved his 'C' much quicker. "Do you think I should post the video?"

"Yes, but don't tell anyone. I want to see how long it takes your family to figure it out."

"And yours. Your mom and sister have the link too. Your dad is probably wondering when I'm going to ask you."

"You talked to Dad two weeks ago when we were there?"

Cade kissed me at the junction of my jaw and ear. "And it nearly killed me to wait."

"You'd think that 2020 would have taught you patience."

"No, it's taught me not to procrastinate. Tomorrow the whole world could change, and while I know I can make it through, I don't want to go it alone." Cade worked his way around to my mouth.

After several engagement-sealing kisses, I pulled back. "Short engagement?"

Cade answered between brief kisses. "The. Shorter. The. Better."

———

On August first, the bears got married in a lovely little ceremony outside of the church on the hill. We got married inside.

The End

ACKNOWLEDGMENTS

There are so many people to thank for their contributions to this book. It was a fun adventure to take with my readers. Thank you to all who contributed or wrote me encouraging notes.

Thanks to Cami who edited each chapter, often late at night, so I could post them in the morning. All of your texts saved me from so many mistakes.

My family, for sharing their home with the fictional characters who often got fed better than they did. And my husband who encourages me every crazy step of the way and puts up with all my messy spreadsheets.

And to my Father in Heaven for putting these wonderful people, and any I may have forgotten to mention, in my life. I am grateful for every experience and blessing I have been granted.

ABOUT THE AUTHOR

Lorin Grace was born in Colorado and has moved around the country ever since, living in eight states and several imaginary worlds.

Currently, she lives in northern Utah with her husband, four children, and a dog who is insanely jealous of her laptop. When not writing Lorin enjoys creating graphics, visiting historical sites, perusing museums, and reading.

Lorin is an active member of the League of Utah Writers and was awarded Honorable Mention in their 2016 creative writing contest short romance story category. Her debut novel, Waking Lucy, was awarded a 2017 Recommended Read award in the LUW Published book contest. In 2018 Mending Fences with the Billionaire, also received a Recommended Read award.

You can learn more about her, and sign up for her writers club at loringrace.com

www.ingramcontent.com/pod-product-compliance
Lightning Source LLC
Chambersburg PA
CBHW070751120626
46557CB00002B/547

*9 7 8 1 9 7 0 1 4 8 0 8 4 *